His Bride for the Taking

By Tessa Dare

This novella was previously published in *Rogues Rush In, a Regency Duet* by Tessa Dare and Christi Caldwell

His Bride for the Taking
Copyright © 2018 by Tessa Dare
Print Edition

Content Advisories

On my website, I offer content advisories for readers who want or need to avoid potentially distressing content. Examples include (but are not limited to) physical or sexual assault, domestic violence, pregnancy loss, character death, PTSD, child abuse, and other kinds of trauma.

Content advisories may be spoilers.

For content advisories for *His Bride for the Taking* and other books, visit:
www.tessadare.com/content-advisories

His Bride for the Taking

By
Tessa Dare

Chapter 1

It was the first rule of friendship among gentlemen: Never, ever lay a hand on your best friend's sister.

Don't do it. Don't even *think* about it.

Not. One. Finger.

Sebastian Ives, Lord Byrne, had never been one for following rules. But promises? He took those seriously indeed. His friendship with Henry Clayton had been the anchor in his turbulent youth, too valuable to risk. So he'd made a vow to himself, and he'd steadfastly held to it—as best he could, anyhow—for years.

Eleven years.

Eleven *long* years.

More than *four thousand days* of wrestling the temptation to take Mary Clayton in his arms and...

Well, from there the specifics varied.

Suffice it to say, aside from the casual contact necessitated by social convention, he'd never touched her—with one exception. After Henry's funeral, he'd held her for hours as she wept. That didn't count, surely.

But today, Sebastian found himself tempted to break his promise. No, "break" was too weak a word. He wanted to bundle his principles, snap them in two, and grind them to sand beneath his boot.

Damn, she looked lovely in her wedding gown.

Not only lovely, but inexplicably alone.

"Where the devil is your groom?"

"I'm not certain," she said.

He paced the floor of the chapel's tiny annex, averting his gaze from the slope of her neck and the gentle curl of auburn hair that adorned it. "How dare he keep you waiting, the bastard."

"Mr. Perry's not a bastard. He's the legitimate son of a barrister."

"I don't care if he's the Prince of Wales. The man made a promise to you, and he's not here to keep it. That makes him a bastard. A tardy bastard, at that."

"He isn't late, Sebastian." She paused. "He's not coming."

"Impossible."

"It's quite possible. In fact, it's evident. He's not here, and neither is his family." She released her breath in a defeated sigh. "He must have changed his mind at the last moment."

"Changed his *mind?* What sort of idiotic milksop would change his mind about marrying you?"

"One who wanted a different sort of wife, I suppose. Someone less opinionated, more amenable. You of all people know I can be difficult."

Difficult? When it came to Mary, his only difficulty had been keeping his distance.

He supposed he could see why a weaker man might find her intimidating. She'd always been more clever than Sebastian and Henry put together. She was strong and self-reliant, because losing her mother at a young age had given her no other choice.

And she was passionate. If she believed in something, she would argue her case with everything she had, and never back down. She believed that women should have the vote, that prisoners should have better rations, that war widows should have pensions.

And that sons of violent drunkards should never spend Christmas alone.

Any man who'd let her go was a bloody fool.

"It's done," she said. "I'll have to find the curate and tell him the wedding has been called off."

"Oh no, you won't. I'm going to go out and find that black-guard and drag him here."

"I don't want to marry a man who needs to be dragged to the altar. Even in my current state of bruised pride, I think I deserve a bit better than that."

"Of course you do. You always deserved better than Giles Perry in the first place. But he proposed to you, and you accepted him. And I'll be damned if he'll get away with this."

"Sebastian."

He relented. "Very well. I won't drag him back. I'll *invite* him to make good on his word to you."

"And if he doesn't accept that invitation?"

Sebastian stopped pacing and turned to her, staring directly into her brilliant blue eyes. "Then I'll call the bastard out."

⌇

"A duel?" Mary's heart missed a beat. "Oh, no. You can't."

"Oh, yes. I will."

He gave her the classic Sebastian look, commanding and stubborn in equal measures. She'd watched grown men wither under that glare. It didn't help that he was built like a Viking warrior, tall and broad-shouldered, with features struck from bronze. There was nothing soft on him, anywhere.

Not on the outside, at least.

"That look doesn't work on me," she said. "I know you too well."

"You don't know everything, Mary."

"I know I've watched you cradle a sparrow hatchling in your hand and feed it from a tincture dropper."

He tipped his head back and groaned. "That was ages ago."

"Mashed worms, three times an hour, for *days.*"

"Rescuing the thing was not my idea. It was Henry's."

"But you were the one who saw it through. The dear little bird thought you were its mother. Remember?" She hooked two fingers and skipped them up his arm. "Hop, hop, hop…"

"Stop."

She withdrew her hand. "I'm just saying that if you ever had any hope of intimidating me, it disappeared that summer. So don't even think about dueling. You're not a man who'd kill another in cold blood."

"Your honor must be defended. Perry's already put off this wedding twice."

"He put off the wedding once," she corrected. "The other time I was in mourning. That wasn't his fault."

"No, that wasn't his fault," Sebastian said in a low, bitter voice. "It was mine."

Mary silently cursed herself. She never should have mentioned it. "You must stop blaming yourself. It was war; men die. You weren't responsible for Henry's decision to enlist."

"Perhaps not. But when he was killed, I became responsible for you."

"I'm nearly twenty-eight years old. I should think by now I'm responsible for myself. And I may have been jilted, but I'm not heartbroken. Giles and I held each other in esteem, but it wasn't a love match. I'll survive."

"Yes, but your reputation will not. You know the things people say when a long engagement is broken. They will assume that you've… Well, that the two of you…" He churned the air with one hand. "Help me here. What's a polite way to say it?"

Mary was suddenly curious about the impolite ways to say it. But that wasn't a conversation for the moment. "They'll assume we anticipated the wedding vows."

"Yes," he said with obvious relief. "That."

"I can't help it if people gossip."

"You'll be ruined. You don't have the money or connections to overcome even a hint of scandal. If you don't marry Perry today, you might never wed anyone at all."

"I'm aware of that." *Painfully so.*

Spinsterhood wasn't an especially appealing prospect—not only because she'd always dreamed of falling in love, setting up house, and having children—but because with Henry gone, the modest family fortune had passed to a third cousin. Thus far, her cousin had been both sympathetic and generous, but should he change his mind, her financial situation could quickly turn grim.

"And what about your political causes and all those charitable organizations?" he asked. "I know how important they are to you. If you lose your good reputation, you'd lose a good measure of influence, too."

Yet another blow, and one that struck nearer her heart.

She shrugged, trying to appear nonchalant. "Perhaps I'll have to surrender my membership in the Ladies' Social Justice Society. The meetings were rather a bore, anyhow."

"I'll take care of this," he said. "Once I have him staring into the end of my pistol, he'll reconsider. Don't worry."

Don't *worry?* The only emotion she could feel at the moment was worry. The chances of Giles killing Sebastian in a duel were slim, but they weren't nonexistent.

"Sebastian, I won't let you risk your life for me. Not over this."

"I'd *give* my life for you. Without a moment's thought."

Goodness. For once, she was caught without a response. He'd taken her breath away. She'd already lost her father, then her only brother.

Mary couldn't bear to lose him, too.

"Listen to me. I'm not going to wed Giles. Ever. Even if you found him, reduced him to pleading at gunpoint, and brought him back to this chapel within the next quarter-hour, I would refuse. Do you mean to threaten me with a pistol, too?"

"Of course not," he grumbled. "I can't force you to marry him."

"Well, then. That's settled. Spinsterhood it shall be." She steadied herself. "If you'll excuse me, I'll go explain to the curate."

He caught her by the arm. "No, I will not excuse you. You will not go explain to the curate. You will not be ruined, and you are not going to be a spinster, either. You're going to marry me."

Chapter 2

Sebastian didn't expect that she would take his declaration well.

And he was right.

"What?" she exclaimed.

"You need to marry someone, and if you won't wed Perry, you will marry me. It's the only way."

Her brow crinkled. "It's not the only way."

"It's the only way I'll allow. I know how small your dowry is. You're not going to be an impoverished spinster if I can help it. And I can."

"If it's the money you're concerned about, you could settle a few thousand pounds on me. You certainly have it to spare."

"And make you a target for unscrupulous fortune-hunters? The devil I will."

"My goodness. What a low opinion you have of my ability to choose suitors."

He stepped back and made a show of searching the room. "The last man you chose to wed isn't here."

He saw her flinch, and he regretted his harsh tone. He didn't want to hurt her. She deserved to be courted by scores of men and worshipped by the lucky fellow she chose. But the world they lived in wasn't fair. That damned Perry would go on to have a fine life, and Mary would pay the price—with her prospects, her reputation, her friends, her influence.

She sighed. "I know you see this as your problem to solve, with Henry gone. But Henry cared about you, too. He wouldn't want you to throw your future away out of misplaced loyalty."

"My loyalty is not misplaced. In fact, there is nowhere else my loyalty *could* be placed. I don't have anyone else." He forged on, wanting to escape the softness in her eyes. "As for the suggestion that I'd be throwing away my future, I won't even dignify that with a response."

"I'm not helpless, Sebastian."

"I know you aren't. But it's what's best. No one will fault you. It's exactly something society would expect me to do, kidnapping a bride from the altar. I'm a shameless rogue."

"No, you're not."

He refused to take up that argument. "You'll be a lady. A wealthy one. I've always known I'd need a wife eventually."

"But…I'm too old," she blurted out.

"You're not old."

"I'm older than you."

"By two years."

"Closer to three. Most men want a younger bride."

"I'm not most men."

She looked at him and sighed. "Yes, I'd noticed."

Well, he'd done more than notice Mary. She'd captured his attention from the very first, and all *because* she was older. She was more worldly and interesting than the girls his own age. Not to mention, her womanly figure had been a source of both temptation and torment.

And on that subject…

"There's one thing you should know," he said. "I am a lord, even if a disgraced one. There's still an entail on the family property." He paused. "I'll need a son. And that means we'll have to…" He searched once again for a polite term.

"Share a bed."

"Do you know what that involves?" He assumed that someone would have given her some idea, but he wanted to be absolutely certain that she knew what she'd be undertaking.

For Sebastian, of course, the bedding would be no chore. He'd imagined making love to her more than once.

Who was he fooling? He'd imagined it hundreds of times. He'd even *dreamed* about her, long after he thought he'd ceased dreaming of anything.

"I understand the marriage bed," she said in perfect innocence. "The husband kisses the wife on the lips, and then she becomes pregnant."

He stared at her, quietly panicked.

She broke into laughter. "I know how intercourse works, Sebastian. Even if I haven't experienced it yet."

Thank God. "So you understand that in order to create a child, we'll need to … do that. At least once. Possibly several times. Even then, the child could be a girl. In which case, we'd have to begin all over again. But I promise, I'd impose on you no more than necessary, and only when you're ready."

She shook her head. "You are running so far ahead of yourself, you're a vanishing dot on the horizon. Right now, I need to announce that *this* wedding isn't happening. After an appropriate interval—a few months, at the least—we can discuss this again. If you still feel the same, and if I agree, we can announce an engagement then. Maybe a wedding in October."

"Unacceptable."

"Christmas, then."

"Definitely not." He'd managed to talk her into this. He wasn't giving her months of time to change her mind. "We're getting married today."

❧

"Today?" Mary echoed. He'd flown past determined, straight into the realm of deranged.

He made a circuit of the vestry, gathering her things. Flowers, veil, wrap. "Your trunks are packed, I assume."

"They're outside, in the coach that Giles hired. We were going to leave for the honeymoon directly after the wedding." Thank goodness they'd planned for a small ceremony at the church, with no wedding breakfast. At least there weren't many witnesses to her humiliation.

"So that's sorted. And you're wearing a gown."

"We *can't* marry today," she declared, having recalled that she was the daughter of a solicitor and claimed more than a passing familiarity with the law. "We don't have a license, and no banns have been read. It simply isn't possible. So there you have it."

He stopped and considered this. "You're right, we'll need a special license. Which means we'll go to Canterbury and be married there."

"Oh, Lord. You've taken leave of your senses. This explains so much."

"My parents are both dead, as are yours. And now Henry, too. We don't have families to attend the ceremony. Or to object."

"*I* object." She spread her arms. "Here I am, standing right in front of you. Objecting."

"You're not objecting on any reasonable grounds. You're just being contrary."

"Well, you're just being hot-headed."

"I'm not hot-headed. I make swift decisions, often ruthless ones. The estate would have gone insolvent years ago otherwise.

But when I heed my gut, I've never had cause to regret it."

She raised an eyebrow. "Yet."

He took her by the hand and fairly dragged her out the vestry's side door, hurrying her toward the waiting coach. "I have a seaside property. A mere cottage, but it's situated nicely on the cliffs near Ramsgate, just a few hours' journey from Canterbury. It's the ideal place to spend a week or two away from London. Less gossip that way."

The gossip.

Heavens, there would be so much gossip.

Well, if there was going to be gossip about her, Mary supposed she would vastly prefer gossip about how she'd been kidnapped by a shameless, sensual rogue, rather than gossip about how she'd been abandoned at the altar by the milquetoast son of a barrister. Passionate was better than pitiful.

"If we leave now," he said, "we'll arrive at the cottage by nightfall. I came here on Shadow, so I'll ride out. But I'll be alongside the coach every step of the way."

He handed her into the carriage, then conferred with the coachman. Bribing him handsomely, she supposed. He was always a man who acted decisively, but she'd never seen him so resolved. Not since he'd declared that he'd purchased a lieutenancy and meant to go off to war.

She flung open the carriage door. "Sebastian, wait."

He reluctantly turned back.

"What about love?" she asked him quietly. "Don't you want to marry for love?"

"I'd rather marry someone I trust."

"Love and trust go hand-in-hand."

"Not in my family, they didn't."

Mary's heart ached for him. The first time he'd come home with Henry from school, he'd been so mistrustful and withdrawn.

Wearing so much invisible armor, it practically clinked as he walked. Over the years, he'd grown comfortable in their home, revealing more and more of himself. Letting down his guard.

But after the war—after Henry died—everything had changed. He'd walled himself away again. She didn't know how to reach him, and she worried he'd never let anyone else draw close enough to try.

"You're being so good to me," she said. "I appreciate it, more than you know. But you needn't do this. I may find I'm well-suited to being a spinster. Or perhaps someone will care enough to wed me despite the scandal."

"Someone already does, Mary. You're looking at him."

In the silence that followed his words, they were both very still.

"If you think I'm being selfless, let me assure you I'm not. I could not keep Henry alive, and that failure will haunt me until I die. You *must* allow me to protect you, or I won't know how to live with myself. You'll have my title and my wealth at your disposal. As a lady of means, you can champion any cause you desire. Aside from giving me an heir, your life will be your own. Let me protect you. That's all I ask."

How could she say no to that? Mary rummaged through her mind for one last objection, but came up empty-handed.

No, not empty-handed. Sebastian's hand was in hers. If she married him, she wouldn't be alone. And neither would he.

Good heavens. She was truly going to be Mary Ives, Lady Byrne.

She gave his hand a squeeze before releasing it. "Take care on the road."

It wasn't quite the wedding Mary had expected.

No, it was much grander. And far more romantic.

Even with a rushed elopement, no guests, and a wedding gown crumpled from travel, the setting was undeniably enchanting. The soaring beauty of the cathedral, the solemn priest in his vestments, the spicy fog of incense. Fading sunlight shone through the stained glass windows, sending crescents of blue and red gliding across the floor.

The scene felt magical, timeless.

And she had the handsomest groom. Sebastian had never looked finer. He fit right into the medieval setting. Like a knight in invisible armor, ready to take on an impossible quest. Mary wasn't certain of her role in this story. Was she the fair maiden he sought to please, or was her broken engagement merely a dragon he needed to slay? His hardened jaw gave no clues.

As the priest began the ceremony, the words washed over her in a hushed murmur.

Sebastian's part came first, and he nearly stepped on the priest's words with his firm, "I will." No hesitation.

Then the priest turned to her. "Mary Elizabeth Clayton, wilt thou have this man to thy wedded husband, to live together after God's ordinance in the holy estate of matrimony?"

She nodded. Thus far, everything sounded acceptable.

"Wilt thou obey him…"

Oh, dear.

"…and serve him…"

She cringed.

"…love, honor, and keep him, in sickness and in health; and, forsaking all others, keep thee only unto him, so long as ye both shall live? If so, answer, 'I will.'"

Mary hesitated.

"If so," the priest repeated, leaning on the words, "answer, 'I

13

will.'"

She couldn't say it. Not quite yet.

She addressed Sebastian directly. "I don't have to do this, you know. I do have a choice."

"What choice? To be a ruined spinster surviving on a meager income?"

"It wouldn't be so bad as you're implying. At least I'd be free to do as I like."

"Mary," he said in a low voice, "this is not the time to argue for the sake of arguing."

"I'm not arguing. Just listen to me for a moment, will you?"

"I don't see the point in discussion."

"Well, I see the point in it," she said, affronted. "When I have something to say, I'd like to be heard. Especially by the man who'll be my husband."

"There's no way in hell I'm taking you back to—"

"Ahem." The priest looked perturbed. "Shall we return to the ceremony?"

"I'm paying for a new chapel," Sebastian snapped. "You can wait until my bride and I are finished speaking."

Mary found his gruff protectiveness oddly endearing, especially since it came under the imminent threat of damnation.

"I'm making a choice, Sebastian. That's all I meant to say. When I make these vows, I'm choosing to do so freely. I'm choosing this." She lowered her voice to a whisper. "I'm choosing *you*."

The casual observer would never notice it, but Mary knew her words had a profound effect. The tension left his shoulders, and suddenly his flinty eyes weren't quite so stern.

For the moment, at least, the warrior had lowered his shield.

She looked at the priest. "I'm ready now."

"If so, answer, 'I will.'"

She looked into her groom's eyes. "I will."

The remainder of the ceremony was brief, in part because there were no rings. Sebastian didn't even have a signet ring. He would have never worn anything of his father's, and most especially not that.

There were vows and a prayer or two, and before Mary even knew it, the thing was over.

"I pronounce you man and wife."

It was done. They were married.

Sebastian leaned forward as though he would kiss her, but then he seemed to change his mind. She might have suspected he'd lost his nerve, if she didn't know Sebastian to be entirely composed of nerve to begin with.

Instead of kissing her lips, he brushed a kiss to her cheek and then rested his temple against hers. A tender gesture, somehow more intimate than a kiss.

"I'll take care of you," he whispered. "Always."

"I know you will," she whispered back.

Mary had no doubt in her mind whatsoever that Sebastian would provide for her every need and guard her with his life.

But it was probably going to knock him on his arse when he learned that she intended to do the same. He needed understanding, warmth, family, love—and she needed all those things, too. This was not going to be a practical arrangement, nor a way for him to satisfy his conscience.

This was going to be a marriage.

And that marriage started tonight.

Chapter 3

By the time they left Canterbury, daylight was fading and thunderclouds had gathered on the horizon. The coachman was not pleased when Sebastian told him they'd be traveling on to Ramsgate in foul weather, but a few guineas made a marked improvement in his mood.

Halfway through the journey, both night and rain were falling. Then Sebastian's horse threw a shoe, slowing their progress to a walk. When they finally arrived at the cottage, the windows were dark. No one came out to greet them. Country hours, he supposed. Perhaps folk went to bed at sundown hereabouts.

Sebastian dismounted Shadow and saw the weary gelding settled in the stable—which looked and smelled as though it hadn't been used in years. Fortunately, the horse had been fed and watered in Canterbury. Any hay in the loft would surely be rotted.

After seeing to his horse, Sebastian pounded at the cottage's front door.

No answer.

Naturally, he had a key to the place, but he didn't carry the thing on his person. It was in a strongbox underneath the desk in his London town house. When he'd left the house this morning, he'd expected to sit quietly seething in a church while he watched Mary wed another man. He never could have imagined that by nightfall he'd be standing in front of this stone cottage on the coast of Kent, having married her himself.

When another round of knocking produced no response, he rattled the door to judge the strength of the bolt. It was already loose—a fact that would have angered him, had the circumstances been different. Tonight, however, this particular instance of shoddy upkeep was a gift. One swift kick, and the bolt gave way.

That accomplished, he darted back to the coach. First he needed to untie Mary's trunks from the carriage and bring them in before they were completely drenched. After he'd stashed her luggage inside the cottage, he returned to the coach for her.

"Put your hands around my neck," he shouted through the rain. "I'll carry you."

"I can walk."

Sebastian didn't have time for this. He hefted her out of the coach without further discussion, tucking her against his chest and carrying her into the cottage.

"You didn't have to do that," she said, once he'd set her down.

"The ground was wet and muddy."

She smiled wryly. "I'm not too concerned about the hem of my gown. It's not as though I'm going to wear it again."

"It's our wedding night," he said. "On the wedding night, the groom carries the bride over the threshold. As hasty and patched-up as the whole thing has been, and considering that you didn't have so much as a ring, I thought I'd do that one thing properly."

"Sebastian. That's terribly sweet."

Sweet, she called him? Good God.

Outside, the coachman snapped the reins and drove off into the night.

Sebastian shoved the door closed and propped it shut with a chair. Mary located a flint and used it to light a candle, giving them their first proper look around the cottage.

Sebastian cursed. It was a shambles. He'd seen henhouses in more habitable condition.

"How long has it been since you visited this place?" she asked.

"Years. But there's supposed to be a caretaker living here with his wife. At least, I've been paying a caretaker's wages. I didn't expect the place to be sparkling, but this?" He batted at a cobweb.

"At least we're out of the rain."

Except that they weren't truly out of the rain. When he looked up at the leaking thatch roof, a cold rivulet of water hit him square in the eye.

Not a few hours ago, he'd stood before a man of God and vowed to keep and protect Mary for so long as they both shall live. He wasn't off to a smashing start.

"We'll go to an inn for the night," he said.

"How? The coachman already left. Shadow's thrown a shoe. And I don't recall seeing an inn when we passed through the village."

"Well, we can't stay here."

"It's only a few leaks, some dust and cobwebs." She scouted around the place, holding her candle high. "This room off the kitchen isn't so neglected. It's dry, at least. And there's a bed. I have fresh bed linens and a quilt in my trunks. They're part of my trousseau."

He slicked back his wet hair. "At least let me walk to the village and find us something to eat."

"Oh, no you won't. You are not leaving me alone in this place." She picked up a hamper he'd unloaded from the coach and set it on the kitchen table. "Giles's sister said she'd packed us a little something. Well, not *us*, but you know."

Yes. Sebastian knew. And he hated the thought that if she'd married that prig she'd be warm, dry, and fed right now.

She opened the hamper. "We have a bottle of wine. That's

promising. And…" She unwrapped a packet of brown paper. "Cake."

Sebastian looked at it. That wasn't merely cake.

That was *wedding* cake.

Suddenly, he wasn't hungry.

She broke off a hunk of cake and took a healthy bite. "We'll survive until the morning," she mumbled with a full mouth. "It will be fine."

He supposed they didn't have much choice.

"Are you sure you don't want some?" She took another bite of cake, then licked her fingers. "It's good."

He shook his head. "I'll lay a fire. You make up the bed."

While she unbuckled the straps on her trunk to search for the bed linens, Sebastian removed his coat and undid his cuffs, turning his sleeves up to the elbow. He searched the kitchen for firewood and found a paltry number of logs. Nowhere near enough to keep a blaze fueled through the night.

He ventured out into the rain and made his way around the cottage's exterior until he found a depleted woodpile beneath a crumbling lean-to. The wood atop the stack was damp. Much of the rest was rotting.

When he got his hands on that caretaker, he would make the man pay for leaving his property in such a state of neglect.

He scavenged a few of the driest logs from the heap, carried them to the chopping block, and gripped the ax handle to pry it free. He braced his feet in the mud and gave it his best one-handed pull. Instead of the blade coming free of the block, the handle broke off in his hand. Sebastian stumbled backward and fell on his arse.

Brilliant. Now he was soaked with rain *and* coated with mud. He carried his armful of unsplit wood back into the cottage and stood in the entry, shaking himself like a dog and sending muddy droplets in all directions. He pried off his boots before crouching at the hearth to make a fire.

With a bit of work, he'd built a respectable blaze. Toasty warmth spread through the kitchen. If they left the door to the bedchamber open, the heat ought to be sufficient to warm that room, too.

"The bed is ready," she said from behind him.

He added a log to the fire, then rose and turned.

Christ.

Mary stood before him wearing a sheer, lacy, snow-white negligee.

He couldn't speak. The cat had got not only his tongue, but every other part of his body that wasn't his eyes, heart, blood, or stiffening cock.

Eleven years, four thousand days. And on how many of those four thousand nights had he imagined her naked? More than he'd ever admit. And here she was, standing before him, wearing the silk equivalent of a branch and a fig leaf.

More beautiful than in his wildest imaginings.

She'd unpinned and brushed out her hair, and the glossy auburn locks tumbled about her shoulders in waves. The wine had stained her lips claret red.

And her nipples were a blushing, rosy pink. He'd always dreamed they'd be pink. He'd also always dreamed they would taste like custard tarts, which now struck him as oddly specific.

"What," he finally scraped out, "is *that?*"

"It's…a nightgown."

"It's a cobweb. There are more holes than thread. You're shivering already." *Not to mention, your rosy nipples are hard as darts.* "Don't you have something more drab and sensible?"

She wrapped her arms about herself. "They're all like this."

Of course they were all like that. She'd packed for a honeymoon. A honeymoon with someone else.

He was a monster. She had to be cold, exhausted, and awash with conflicted emotions. Even if her heart wasn't broken, it must have been bruised. From the looks of that negligee, she might have even been looking forward to her wedding night with Perry. Instead, she was here in an infested, rotting hellhole. With him.

And he was berating her about her choice of sleeping apparel.

Well done, Sebastian. Well done, indeed.

She crossed the room to him. "Come, then. Off with your clothes." She yanked the hem of his shirt from his trousers.

"Mary." He took a step in retreat. "I'm not... We're not... Not tonight."

She tipped her head to the side and regarded him. "You are soaked to the skin and spattered with mud. I'm not being a brazen hussy, I'm protecting my embroidery. I worked hard on those bed linens, you know. So take off your things and leave them to dry by the fire."

He shook his head. "I'll sleep on the floor."

"Don't be absurd. I won't let you sleep on the floor."

"It's nothing. I slept in much rougher conditions while on campaign."

"This isn't the army, Sebastian. There's a perfectly good bed."

"Exactly. Bed, singular. Not beds."

"We *are* man and wife," she teased. "The priest said so."

Wife.

She was his *wife.*

"I know you mean to take care of me," she said. "But now that we're married, I get to take care of you, too. You're not sleeping on the floor." She touched his wrist. "Besides, it's cold. I don't want to be alone."

Very well. She had him there.

And in that negligee, she had him hard as granite.

This would be a very long night.

"You go ahead and get in the bed," he said. "Take the side nearest the kitchen. It will be warmest. I'll join you in a minute."

He waited until he heard her slip beneath the quilt before disrobing hastily and draping his wet clothing over two chairs near the fire. As he crept into the bedchamber, he tried to stay in the shadows. Not out of modesty, but so she wouldn't be alarmed. He was a rather hulking fellow, big in all sorts of ways. Experienced women seemed to like his body just fine, but he wasn't certain how a virgin would react.

He stretched out beside her on the bed, crossed his arms over his chest, and closed his eyes.

She nestled up against him.

He wriggled a few inches away.

She snuggled close again. "Hold me. You're so warm. And I can't stop shivering."

With a heavy sigh, he draped one arm around her shoulders, still careful to keep their bodies apart from the navel down. "I don't want to crush you."

"How could you crush me? You're next to me, not atop me."

He groaned. *Don't give me ideas.*

"You're inching away again," she accused. "Am I so objectionable?"

"The furthest thing from it."

"Then what's the matter?"

Fine. Don't say you didn't ask for it.

He rolled onto his side to face her, pulled her close, and thrust his rampant arousal against her belly. "There. I hope that answers your question."

She swallowed hard. "Oh. Were you wanting to—"

"Engage in politely phrased activities? No." He released her. "Not at all."

"You don't have to be so vehement about it."

"A man's body has a mind of its own. Especially when the man in question is naked and in bed with a beautiful woman. One clad in nothing but a wisp of lace, who keeps wriggling her body against his." He exhaled heavily. "But I don't want you to be anxious. We'll wait until you're ready. Whether that means weeks, months, even years. I won't rush you."

She was silent for a moment. And then she started to laugh.

"What?"

"You won't rush me?" The bed quaked with her laughter. "This from the man who kidnapped me in the morning, married me in the afternoon, and installed me in his remote seaside cottage by evening. But you won't *rush* me. Oh, Sebastian. That is too much."

He didn't know what to say.

"Look at that furrow in your brow." She rubbed the space between his eyebrows, as though attempting to iron it flat. "Don't look so stern. I'm only teasing you. But perhaps you're not ready to be teased. I won't rush you, either."

Without thinking, he reached out to stroke her hair.

She laid her head on his chest. "I've worried about you in the past year. You're too stubborn to let on, but I know you've been hurting. Whether it's Henry or the war, or something I can't even comprehend. Even when we're in the same room, you've seemed so far away."

He didn't know how to answer that. It was true, he'd been grieving. Not only for Henry, but for so many of his brothers in arms. But it wasn't something he knew how to talk about. And he could scarcely complain to Mary about it. She'd lost her only brother. With both her parents gone, Henry had been her only family remaining. She was alone.

Or rather, she'd *been* alone. Now she was with him.

"Go to sleep," he told her. "At first light, I'm taking you away from this miserable place."

She tilted her head to look up at him. "Kiss me goodnight?"

He hesitated.

"It's our wedding night. It seems we should at least have that. For tradition's sake, if nothing else."

Very well. He touched his lips to hers, giving her a chaste, sweet kiss.

And then, Devil take him, the kiss became more.

His first taste of her was a rich, buttery sweetness. Like cake. That cursed wedding cake that was meant for her to share with another man. He wanted to steal that taste from her mouth and burn it to ash.

He swept his tongue between her lips. Exploring, claiming. He slid his hand to the back of her head and wove his fingers into her hair, tilting her face to his to deepen the kiss. She pressed closer, and the exquisite softness of her body made his skin tighten and his blood pound.

Within him, desire sparked and spread like a blaze.

Natural. Wild. Uncontrolled.

This was meant to be a goodnight kiss. A sweet brush of lips against lips before drifting off to sleep. Instead, his long-buried desires were waking and stretching. Roaring to life with a ferocity that startled even him.

He yearned to explore every part of her with his hands. Cup her breasts in his palms, run his fingers along her sweet, hot cleft. He wanted her beneath him. Astride him. Pressed against the wall. Bent over the table, with all that frothy lace pushed up to her waist.

He wanted her calling his name, holding him tight. He wanted-ed to fall asleep tangled with her, and wake up with her in his arms.

He wanted all she had to give him, and more.

Mary, Mary.

A crash of timber and iron jolted them both. The kiss came apart, but he kept Mary close.

Two human silhouettes filled the doorway between the bed-chamber and the kitchen.

"Whoever ye are," came a menacing voice, "ye'd best prepare to die."

Chapter 4

In the chilling darkness, Mary clutched Sebastian tight. Her heart trilled like a rabbit's in her chest.

Pushing the quilt aside, Sebastian let her slip from his arms and quietly swung his legs to the side of the bed. She sensed his muscles coiling with tension.

He was preparing to fight.

"Don't be frightened," he murmured. "I'll keep you safe."

She exhaled shakily. Of course he would fight to keep her safe—he was so damnably selfless that way—but she needed *him* to be safe, too.

As she blinked, her eyes adjusted to the dim, flickering firelight. The two silhouettes in the door belonged to a man and a woman. The man brandished a long, round-barreled weapon. A rifle.

Be careful, Sebastian.

The man leveled his weapon.

Sebastian rose to his full, imposing height, moving between Mary and the door. Into the line of fire.

He gave the intruders a single, thunderous word. *"Begone.'*

"Lord preserve us." The man's weapon shook. Out of fearful trembling, she suspected, not anger. She squinted and peered around Sebastian's torso. For heaven's sake, it was nothing more dangerous than a broom handle.

"What sort of devil be ye?"

"I should be asking you that."

"'Tis a demon, to be sure," the woman said. "Naked as sin. Formed like Lucifer 'imself."

"Get the hell out," Sebastian said, each word a distinct threat. "Both of you. Or I'll snap your miserable necks with my bare hands."

For a tense moment, no one moved.

Finally, the broomstick-wielding man broke the silence. "Have at 'im, Fanny."

The woman rushed forward, wailing like a Valkyrie and raising a blunt cudgel over her head—one that appeared, from Mary's eyes, to be a rolling pin.

She thwacked Sebastian in the arm. "Take that, ye foul devil's spawn. Back to the fire and brimstone with ye."

Sebastian, clearly unwilling to strike out at a woman, ducked and raised his arms to protect his head. He turned his back to her.

Fanny skittered around him in circles, battering him about the shoulders. "Have that." *Thump.* "And that." *Thwack.* "I rebuke thee."

Meanwhile, the man remained in the doorway, apparently content to let his female counterpart do the fighting for them both.

Well, Mary decided two women could play at this game.

She leapt from the bed and launched herself at the woman, tackling her against the wall. "Stop that, you shrieking harpy."

"Get off me, ye demon's consort. Cavorting with the Devil in my man's and I's bed."

"That's no devil." Mary found the woman's ear and gave it a tweak. "That's your master you're bludgeoning."

Fanny gasped. She flung aside the rolling pin, and from Sebastian's pained shout, Mary deduced the thing had bounced off his toes.

"God keep us," Fanny breathed. "Dick, 'tis Lord Byrne 'imself."

"Y-yer lordship." The man in the door—Dick, she supposed—pulled the hat from his head and bowed. "Dick Cross. I'm the caretaker. And this is the missus, Fanny. We hadn't expected ye. A thousand apologies, milord."

"A thousand isn't nearly enough." Sebastian whipped the quilt from the bed and wrapped it about his hips. "Try multiplying that by a factor of a hundred."

Dick shuffled his feet. "Ciphering were never my strong point, milord."

Ignoring him, Sebastian went to Mary. "Are you hurt?"

"No. Not at all."

He turned to the caretaker and his wife. "That's a stroke of luck for the two of you."

"We'll leave ye alone, then." Fanny gathered up her rolling pin and inched toward the door, tugging her husband with her. "Ever so sorry to have interrupted yer night of sin."

"It's not a night of sin."

"We'll leave straightaway and let you be with yer lady of the evening."

Sebastian puffed with anger. "What are you—"

"Now, now. No shaming from our quarter," she added. "Only God can judge. Perhaps fornication's forgiven for the upper classes. Special dispensations from the Church, no doubt."

"Must say, she's a fair one," Dick put in. "A sight better than the wenches what walk the docks."

Fanny whacked her husband with the rolling pin. "What would ye know about the wenches what walk the docks?"

"Let me alone, woman. 'Tis no concern of yours. The master wouldn't truck with that sort. Got the quality goods, he has."

"Enough." Sebastian grabbed the caretaker by the shirt and

lifted him onto his toes. "Insult my wife one more time, and I will shove that broomstick up your arse."

"Y-yer…" His eyes flicked to Mary. "Yer wife?"

"Yes. My wife. Lady Byrne. As of today."

"Beggin' apologies, milord. Milady. We didn't receive any word that ye'd married. Nor a notice that ye planned to be in residence."

"I can see by the state of this cottage that you didn't. Not that it's any excuse. Imagine my displeasure when I bring my bride for a seaside honeymoon, only to find the place in complete disarray. You ought to keep the house in readiness at all times. Instead, we arrived to find this place filthy and in disrepair."

"We've been feelin' poorly."

"Oh, I'll teach you what it is to feel poorly."

Mary decided to intervene. She laid a hand to his arm, gently. "Sebastian."

It was enough.

His demeanor softened. He gestured toward the door. "Begone, the both of you."

"Aye, aye. We'll jes' be in the kitchen, then."

"You'll be in the barn," he said. "We'll discuss the state of your employment—or lack of it—tomorrow."

After the couple had left, Mary and Sebastian returned to the bed. He turned her so that her back rested against his chest, spooning his body around hers. Keeping her warm and safe.

Her eyelids grew heavy. Heavens, what a day. It seemed impossible to bend her mind around it all. A jilting, an elopement, a decrepit honeymoon cottage.

And one fiery, passionate kiss. If a single kiss could create such a whirlwind of sensation, she could only imagine how their lovemaking would be. It boded well for the honeymoon, she thought. If only they hadn't been interrupted.

Mary pressed her lips together, trying not to giggle. In the end, she couldn't help it. She dissolved into laughter.

"What?"

"The rolling pin. The ciphering. Everything."

"It's not amusing."

"To the contrary. It's highly amusing. I've never been called a demon's consort before. You'll be laughing about it tomorrow."

"Doubtful."

"Very well. Perhaps you'll be laughing about it next year." *Or maybe the decade after that.*

"Go to sleep," he grumbled.

Just this once, she decided to obey his command.

Chapter 5

M ary was first to wake. The fire in the kitchen had gone cold, so she wriggled backward, curling into the heat of his body. He growled a little in his sleep. The hard, hot ridge of his erection jutted against her thigh. Apparently, one part of him was awake. A large part.

Her own intimate places softened. She felt a keen, hollow ache of curiosity.

Slowly, stealthily, she turned to face him, trying to muster the courage to steal a peek under the quilt. However, her carnal investigations were set aside when she glimpsed his face.

He looked so different in his sleep. Less troubled, more vulnerable. She stroked the thick, tawny hair back from his brow.

There it was, the tiny sunburst scar just beneath his hairline.

She remembered the night he'd been given that wound. Mary had been the only one awake, sitting in the kitchen with a cup of tea and reading over some papers. Sebastian had stumbled into the house well past midnight, his eye blackened and blood streaming from his hairline down to his chin.

Mary had set her work aside at once. She'd cleaned his wounds and applied a poultice to his blackened eye. He'd told her he'd been in a fight—someone he knew from Cambridge. But the story was just a story. He knew she'd noticed the remarkable similarity between the sunburst cut on his brow and the sunburst shape of his father's signet ring.

And she knew Sebastian had noticed the work that kept her up late. She'd been correcting the errors in contracts her father had drawn up for a client. That was the time when his mind had just begun to fail.

They had these little secrets, the two of them. Always unspoken, and yet always understood.

She pressed a kiss to his scar.

He stretched and yawned, then turned to stare up at the roof above. "I was hoping this cottage had been a nightmare." He rose from bed and went to retrieve his trousers. "I'm going to walk Shadow into the village and find the smithy. Once he's been shoed, I'll ride back and we'll leave for Ramsgate at once." He pulled his shirt over his head. "Stay abed. Get some more sleep."

Mary nodded in drowsy agreement and drew the quilt up to her chin.

However, the moment the door closed behind him, she jumped out of bed. She excavated her simplest, plainest frock from the depths of her trunk, dressed in haste, and had a look around the cottage.

Last night, she hadn't explored any of it, aside from the kitchen and the small room she now understood to be Dick and Fanny's bedchamber.

The cottage wasn't large, and it had been sorely neglected, but with a bit of work it could be a charming home. Downstairs, she explored a parlor with a large fireplace ideal for cozy nights in, and a dining room nowhere near large enough for a party, but more than sufficient for two.

A library rounded out the ground floor, and it was Mary's favorite room yet. Bookshelves covered the walls from floor to ceiling, and a massive mahogany desk lodged by the window, issuing a dare: *Just you try to budge me.*

She'd no desire to make the attempt.

Instead, she took a seat at the desk and ran her palms over the glossy wood. When she inhaled, her lungs filled with the scents of leather and tobacco and old books. A powerful wave of memories crashed through her.

The library was so much like Papa's.

Henry had never taken an interest in the law, but Mary had loved watching their father work. She'd steal out of bed on nights when she couldn't sleep, tiptoeing through the house to his study. There, she'd find him poring over a legal reference or a making notes on a contract. He didn't scold her or chase her back to bed. Instead, he'd take her onto his lap and explain whatever task lay before him—in simple, but never condescending, language.

Her father had believed girls should be educated in all the same subjects as boys, and he'd encouraged Mary to form her own opinions and share them with confidence.

Most importantly, he'd always made time for her.

Sadly, his time on earth had been much too short. She missed him every day.

Swallowing back the lump in her throat, she left the study and made her way up the stairs to explore the cottage's bedchambers. There were three in total. Two small rooms, and a larger one for the master and mistress of the house.

She went to the window and opened it wide. A breathtaking view greeted her. The blue-green sea, frosted with whitecaps and sparkling with sunshine.

Beautiful.

She pressed a hand to her heart. In no time at all, she'd fallen in love with this cottage. It was the perfect place for a honeymoon.

They would not be leaving for Ramsgate today. Not if she had anything to say about it. However, if she meant to convince Sebastian, she had no time to waste.

She went outside and found the well. Once she'd drawn a full pail of water, she took it in both hands and—rather than carrying it inside the cottage—proceeded directly to the barn, where Dick and Fanny Cross lay snoring atop a mound of straw.

She dashed the water over them. "Wake up."

The caretaker and his wife jolted to life, sputtering.

"You will not find me an easy mistress to please," Mary said, "but at the moment I am your best friend. If you want any hope of keeping your posts, you'd best rouse yourselves and prepare to work your fingers to nubs. Do you understand me?"

The caretaker struggled to stand. "Yes, milady."

"Good." She set the bucket at the caretaker's feet. "You can begin by drawing more water and bringing it in to the kitchen. Fanny, gather up brooms, rags, soap, and some vinegar."

Fanny nodded.

"This cottage—or at least a fair part of it—*will* be presentable by the time your lord returns." Mary arched an eyebrow. "Or prepare to face the wrath of the demon's consort."

Within an hour, they had the kitchen swept and the cobwebs knocked from the corners. Mary had scrubbed the panes of the windows with vinegar and a drop of lemon oil. Dick brought in eggs from the henhouse, and Fanny produced bread, a slab of bacon, and some butter. In the cupboard, Mary found a jar of preserves and a locked tea caddy. She broke the rusted lock with a knife and was rewarded with a small stash of serviceable, if a bit stale-looking, tea.

By the time she had the kettle boiling, eggs and bacon frying, and bread sliced for toasting, her hair had begun to come loose, and perspiration dotted her brow. She meant to wash her face and pretty herself before Sebastian returned, but she didn't have a chance. The clop of Shadow's freshly shoed hooves on the lane told her he'd already returned.

She patted her hair, hastily untied her apron and cast it aside. At the last second, she adjusted the bouquet of wildflowers she'd picked on a whim earlier and crammed into a crockery vase.

As Sebastian came through the door, she clasped her hands together and tried not to appear as anxious as she felt inside. How silly, that she'd be nervous. But perhaps it was natural. This was her first morning as a wife, and she found herself eager for her husband's approval. Maybe he'd be impressed by everything she'd accomplished in only a few hours, and then he'd embrace the idea of domestic bliss.

My darling, you've worked a miracle. I can't imagine how I ever lived without you. Truly, you are the best of wives.

"Good morning." She smiled and prepared herself to receive his praise.

Instead, he shook his head. "Mary, what have you done?"

Sebastian gestured broadly at the kitchen. "What is all this?"

As he watched, the smile faded from her face. "It's breakfast," she said. "And we did a bit of tidying up."

The kitchen hadn't merely been "tidied up." It had undergone a complete transformation.

The spiders had been evicted from the corners, and the thick layer of dust had vanished from the fireplace mantel. The smell of fresh sea air breezed through the open window, and a pair of lacy curtains fluttered in the wind. Everything in the place had been scrubbed and polished to a gleam. Even the floor looked to have been scoured.

She must have worked every blessed minute he'd been away. Yet more impressive, it would seem she'd convinced Dick and Fanny Cross to do some labor, too.

The prettiest thing in the room, of course, was Mary herself. She was lovely as a Dutch painting. She'd dressed in a sage-green frock with cap sleeves and delicate lace edging. Her skin seemed to glow in the morning light, and her cheeks had a fetching blush. She wore her auburn hair in a loose, haphazard knot, and stray wisps had curled at her temples and the nape of her neck.

"You look as though someone stomped on your new hat," she said. "Don't you like it?"

"It's not that I don't like it. You shouldn't have put yourself to all this trouble, that's all. We're leaving for Ramsgate this morning."

"Yes, about that…" She chewed her bottom lip. "Let's at least have breakfast first. I'm hungry. And if I'm hungry, you must be starving."

Sebastian *was* starving. He hadn't had a bite to eat since breakfast yesterday, and that might as well have been last year. But since that kiss last night, another sort of hunger was tormenting him. He was ravenous for his wife.

While she loaded a plate for him, he washed his hands. Then he sat down to a feast. Fried eggs, bacon, toasted bread with butter and jam. How had she managed all this?

Eat first, his stomach growled. *Talk later.*

He attacked his food, downing four eggs, two rashers of bacon, and six points of buttered toast in a matter of minutes.

She filled his teacup for the third time. "Feeling human again?"

"Mostly."

When she bent over the table to pour his tea, he could glimpse not only the sweet, abundant curves of her breasts, but the dark, secret valley between them. If he didn't know better, he'd have thought she *meant* to give him the tempting view.

"I've been thinking." She propped an elbow on the table and

rested her chin in her hand. "Instead of going on to Ramsgate, perhaps we could stay here."

"No." He drained his tea and set down the teacup with authority. "We're not going to spend another night in this cottage."

"But—"

"I'm taking you to an inn. Or a hotel. The finest establishment Ramsgate has to offer, whatever that might be."

And wherever they stayed, he would demand the best room. Not merely a room, but a suite. An apartment with a soaking tub and a private dining room.

And, most importantly, separate bedchambers.

Last night, that simple goodnight kiss had nearly been his undoing. This morning he was slavering like a dog, after just one glimpse of her breasts. If he shared a bed with her again tonight, he'd risk losing all control.

"But Ramsgate is so popular this time of year. It will be full to bursting with ladies on holiday. Too many prying eyes. Someone will recognize us, and then the rumors will be all over England."

"Unless we're visiting the shops or the seaside, we won't attract notice."

She laughed to herself. "Sebastian, you are like a walking exhibition of Grecian sculpture. Wherever you go, you attract notice. Once we ride into town together, we may as well put a notice in the *The Times*. Can't we remain here and avoid the gossip? In just one morning, I've already improved the kitchen. Give it a few more days, and this cottage will be positively charming, you'll see."

He relented. "Very well. If that's truly what you want."

"It's what I want. If it weren't, you know I wouldn't hesitate to tell you."

"This is true." He tapped a finger on the table's edge. "But I have one condition. We must do something about our sleeping arrangements."

"I wholeheartedly agree." She pushed back from the table. "Which is why I've something to show you upstairs."

Chapter 6

Sebastian followed her up the stairs, feeling strangely wary. Just what sort of surprise did she have in mind?

"I found it in the attic," she chattered on the way. "It must be centuries old. We dusted it off with rags, and Dick carried it down to this room. It's the largest." She led him into a bedchamber branching off the corridor and made a sweeping arm gesture toward one corner. "See? It's a bed."

Sebastian blinked at the jumble of timbers. "That's not a bed. That's firewood."

"It's a disassembled bed. And I think you'd have a difficult time burning it. It's heavier than bricks." She lifted one end of a plank. "I don't even know what kind of wood this is."

He ran his fingers over the surface and examined the grain. "I'm not certain, either." He picked up a lathe-turned wooden leg. Or was it a finial? Time had coated the wood in a dark, impenetrable patina that he couldn't even gouge with his thumbnail.

"I don't think it's English. What style of carving do you make that out to be?" She leaned close to him, offering a piece decorated with a chain of stylized wildflowers.

He shrugged. "Swedish, maybe?"

"Well, wherever it came from, it's going to be slept in tonight. I already told Fanny to stuff a mattress tick with fresh straw. We just have to put the frame together. All the pieces seem to be here." She took hold of a board and lifted it, eyeing the dimensions. "Do you think this is a slat, perhaps?" She tipped her head to regard it from another angle. "Or a rail?"

With a shrug, she carried it to the center of the room and laid it flat on the floor.

Sebastian poked through the stack of planks and pieces. "Simple mortise and tenon joints. Shouldn't take long." He chose two pieces that looked as though they'd been hewn to fit together, and the tenon slipped into the mortise like a hand into a fitted glove. "That's one joint connected."

Mary paused in the act of laying a second plank next to the first, lining up their bottom edges for comparison. "Oh, no. We're not going about it all higgledy-piggledy. We don't know if those two pieces belong together."

"Of course they do. They were made to fit."

"You can't be sure of that."

He held up the joint for her, sliding the tenon in and out of its slot a few times. "Is that not proof enough?"

"Perhaps there are two that would fit the same hole."

"Well, I don't know how you propose to complete this bed without joining pieces together. Did you find a leaflet in the attic with instructions? In Swedish?"

"Of course I didn't. That's why we need a plan. Now, we're going to arrange all these pieces neatly in rows first, laying them out on the floor so that we can count and compare. We'll put a little mark on the similar ones. Plank A, plank B, and so on. Then we'll chalk up a diagram on the floor and—"

"I thought you wanted to sleep in this bed tonight. Not next week."

"What's wrong with planning first?"

"You're making it more complicated than it needs to be." He lifted the wide, flat headboard and placed it against the wall. "Is this where you want it?"

"A little to the left." She waved him to the side. "No, back to the right a touch. There."

He set the piece down, then returned to the stack of timbers and selected the largest. "This goes at the foot of the bed."

"Are you certain?"

"Yes." He lifted the board with a grunt, swung it about, and positioned it parallel to the headboard. "Hold that in place."

She sounded skeptical. "So you've done this before. Assembled beds."

"Loads of them."

"Loads of them? When and where was that?"

He gave a strangled groan of impatience. "Just trust me, Mary. I have it all under control. This won't take but a few minutes."

One hour later

Mary pulled to a standing position and massaged the wrenched muscle at the small of her back. "It's still not right. That one doesn't go there."

"Yes, it does." As she stood observing, Sebastian tried once again to shove the wooden tab of one rail into the slot carved into a leg.

"See? It doesn't fit."

"It will fit. There aren't any other pieces left that it could be."

"It's probably one of the pieces we've already used. It could be anywhere." She gestured at the half-finished bed frame. "Or maybe the right piece was never here to begin with. This was why I wanted to make a plan, you know."

He gave her a look. "Don't be that way."

"Don't be *what* way? Right?" She huffed a breath, blowing a wisp of hair off her cheek. "There's nothing else to be done. We'll have to take it apart and start over."

He swore with passion. "We are not taking the thing apart. And this piece does fit." He glared at the wood, as though he could force it into submission through the sheer power of masculine brooding. "I just need a mallet."

"I think *I* need a mallet," she grumbled.

"What?"

"Nothing," she chirped with bright innocence. "I'll find you that mallet straightaway."

⟋∿•

Two hours after that

Mary sat in the corner of the bedchamber with her knees hugged to her chest.

With a grimace of effort, Sebastian gave the bed-key one final twist to tighten the ropes. *"There."*

Mary watched as he dragged the freshly stuffed mattress tick onto the frame.

She would have offered to help. But by this point, she knew better than to touch—or even breathe on—his work in progress. And God forbid she make a helpful suggestion.

He stood back, straightened, and used his sleeve to wipe the sweat streaming off his brow. "Finished."

She stared at the bed, biting her tongue.

"Well…?" He propped his hands on his hips. "I told you I'd have it put together."

"Yes, but—"

"But *what,* Mary? But *what?*"

"But there are three boards left over." She stood and pointed. "Where do they go?"

He gave a one-shouldered shrug. "Must be surplus."

"Surplus? What centuries-old bed comes with surplus pieces?"

"This one."

She rubbed her temples.

"It doesn't matter." He took a pace backward. "It's sturdy enough to hold an ox. Just watch."

"Sebastian, wait."

He took two running steps and launched himself at the bed, twisting in midair so that he landed on his back. All sixteen stone of him, squarely plunked in the center of the mattress.

"See?" He folded his hands under his head and gave her a smug look. "I told you it was st—"

Crash.

One side of the bed frame collapsed beneath his weight, tipping the mattress at an angle and shunting him to the floor.

Mary stood very quietly.

He stared blankly at the ceiling. "Go on. Say it."

"Say what?"

"I know you're thinking it. You may as well have out with it."

"I'm not sure what you mean," she lied.

"Yes, you are."

"Let's go downstairs for some tea."

"For the love of God, Mary. I know it's coming. Just say it now."

"I don't—"

"Say it."

"I told you so!" she shouted. "Is that what you want to hear? I told you this would happen. I told you you were doing it wrong. I. Told. You. So."

He stared up at the ceiling, infuriatingly silent.

Mary, however, was only getting started. "I wanted to make a plan. But noooo. You don't need a plan. You've assembled loads of beds. You know exactly which pieces fit where. Because you, like all men, have a magical nugget of furniture-assembly expertise dangling in your left bollock." She flung a hand at the unused boards. *"Surplus?* You're telling me sixteenth-century Swedish artisans made *surplus?"*

He finally pulled himself off the floor. "I"—he jabbed a finger in his chest—"told you"—the finger turned on Mary—"that we should go to Ramsgate. Where they *have* beds already. Assembled beds. Comfortable beds. Beds just sitting there in well-appointed rooms, waiting for someone to use them."

"I don't want to go to Ramsgate."

"Yes, so you told me. You're very keen to avoid the gossip. God forbid you be seen with me in public."

Her chin jerked. "What?"

"I mean, you could have been married to Giles Perry, a barrister's son with a promising political career. Instead, you're with the disgraced Lord Byrne. The one who dirties his hands in trade, because his father drove the estate straight up to the brink of insolvency and only failed to take it over the edge because he drank himself to death first. Those ladies on holiday would cluck their tongues, wouldn't they? All of England would be shaking their heads."

"Sebastian. You can't think I'm ashamed of having married you."

"Of course not," he said mockingly. "You prefer to spend the week squirreled away with me in some ramshackle cottage, scrubbing floors and assembling furniture, when you could be staying in the finest seaside resort."

"I *do* prefer it."

"To be sure." He rolled his eyes to the ceiling. "Why wouldn't you? Just look at all the fun we're having right this very moment."

She shook her head. "I can't believe this."

"Well, I can't believe you. It's clear you're trying to persuade me into remaining here. Vases of flowers on the table, breakfast." He gave the unfinished bed a disgusted look. *"That."*

"Well, pardon me for attempting to make our honeymoon cottage just the tiniest bit romantic."

"It's not supposed to be romantic. You were jilted by your groom. I stepped in to marry you out of loyalty to your brother. It's not as though we clasped hands and ran away into the sunset, Mary." He swept her with a cold look. "We're not in love."

His words struck her in the chest with such force, she couldn't breathe.

And she hadn't any logical reason to feel hurt. He was only speaking the truth. She simply hadn't realized, until this moment, how much she wished the truth were different.

"I..." She blinked rapidly, forcing back a hot tear.

He pushed his hands through his hair and cursed. "Mary, don't listen to me. We're both exhausted, and—"

"It's all right, Sebastian. You don't need to explain." Mary backed her way toward the door. She had to escape this room. The walls were closing in on her, squeezing at her heart. "We can leave for Ramsgate whenever you're ready."

Chapter 7

It took Sebastian about five seconds to realize what a bastard he'd been. However, he forced himself to wait a few hours before attempting to tell her so. She needed time and space to breathe, and so did he.

As penance, he did exactly as she'd suggested from the start.

He took the whole damn bed apart, sorted the pieces by size and function, chalked an outline on the floor, and wouldn't you know. It all fit together as it should.

When he finally went looking for her, she wasn't in the cottage. He searched through every room, growing increasingly concerned, until he returned to the master bedchamber and happened to look out the window. She was down by the water, walking along the sandy shore.

He picked his way down the winding path to the beach. As she came into view, he paused a moment to recover his breath.

Her lovely profile was to him as she stared out over the ocean. The breeze whipped at her filmy summer frock and toyed with the loose strands of her hair. Before she walked on, she stopped and bent to gather something from the sand, adding it to a collection in her palm.

"Mary!" He jogged down the beach until he reached her side. Once he'd reached her, he searched his brain for the right words. Only three came to mind. "I'm a jackass."

She ducked her head. "You're not alone."

They walked on together.

"What is it you're collecting?" he asked.

"Cockleshells." She held them up for him to see. "Couldn't resist."

Mary, Mary, quite contrary, how does your garden grow?
With silver bells and cockleshells, and pretty maids all in a row.

Whenever she dug her heels into an argument, Henry had teased her with that rhyme, even long past the age when they should have outgrown it. Sebastian supposed that was what brothers did.

She poked through her little collection with a fingertip. "Perhaps I'll put them in the garden, with some silver bells and pretty maids all in a row. It would be a nice remembrance, wouldn't it?"

"I think he'd like that. A chance to tease you from beyond the grave."

"Henry did have a point. I've tried to temper my inclination toward contrariness, but it never seems to work. I'm my father's daughter, and it's in my blood. A bit of rousing debate was like a game for us. One we both enjoyed." She gave him a cautious look. "But I know it's not that way in everyone's family."

It certainly hadn't been that way in Sebastian's home. No good-natured arguments between his parents. Only threats and accusations and the sound of china shattering against the wall.

"I'll try to be more patient," he said.

"I'll try not to be right all the time," she teased. "I suppose this means our first argument as a married couple is out of the way."

The knot in his chest unraveled. Apologies accomplished, just like that. He'd learned so much from his time spent in the Clayton house. It was in that house he'd learned to be a man.

Henry had taught him what it meant to be a friend.

Mr. Clayton had taught him what it meant to be responsible.

Mary had taught him what it meant to yearn. To sense there was something more beneath the surface of a friendship. To wish he knew how to bring that into the light. To wonder if he could ever deserve it.

She stopped to gather another cockleshell and turned it over between her fingers, inspecting it. Dissatisfied, she cast it away. "Imagine if I'd married Giles. I would have been 'Mary Perry, quite contrary.' How dreadful."

He pulled a face. "Dreadful, indeed. Why did you accept his proposal if you didn't love him?"

"Considering his political aspirations, I told myself I could do some good as his wife. That was before I realized he was only motivated by ambition. He didn't truly care about serving the people. I'd have gone mad as his wife, trying to hold my tongue in company and support his bland political positions without expressing my own thoughts. I'm so relieved that I didn't have to marry him."

"Are you?"

"Yes. In fact, I'm more than relieved. I'm happy."

Happy.

The word made Sebastian's brain spin.

Naturally, he agreed with the assessment that she and Perry would have made a disastrous match. He'd known that from the first. Differences of opinion aside, the man simply wasn't good enough for her.

But could she truly be *happy* to have been jilted?

That was too much to believe. In all likelihood, she was merely soothing her own feelings. Telling herself it was for the best, in order to ease the pain.

In time, he'd do his best to make her happy in truth.

"I have something for you." He reached into his breast pocket, fishing around for his small gift. "I brought it back from the village, but I forgot about it earlier, what with all the—"

Her eyebrows lifted. "Surplus?"

"Exactly." He smiled a little. "While I was at the smithy with Shadow, I had the blacksmith make this." He withdrew the tiny circle of polished silver and placed it in her palm. "It's only temporary. You'll have something much finer at the first opportunity. But for now, it's the best I could do."

She regarded it wordlessly.

Sebastian shifted his weight from one foot to the other. At the smithy, it had seemed a good idea. Now that he saw it resting in her delicate hand, the ring looked crude and paltry. "You don't have to wear it."

She clamped her fingers over it, closing the ring in her fist. "Certainly I'm going to wear it. Don't think I'll give it back now."

He exhaled with relief.

She slid the thin, humble band onto her third finger. "It was thoughtful of you to bring it." She stretched up to kiss his cheek. "Thank you."

As she pulled back, he wrapped an arm around her, keeping her close. His gaze dropped to her pale-pink lips.

Irresistible.

He kissed her, and she leaned into his embrace. Her frock was wonderfully thin, and her breasts melted against him. He explored her mouth with possessive strokes of his tongue, taking more, and then yet more. She offered everything he asked, and then began to take from him, too. She laced her fingers together at the back of his neck and clung tight, making him her captive.

Love, never set me free.

His hand began to wander of its own accord, sweeping down her spine and over the flare of her hip, coming to settle on the curve of her bottom. He flexed his fingers, claiming a plump handful of flesh and drawing her body to his with a firm, swift motion. His cock grew and stiffened, pulsing against the softness of her belly.

He bent his head and kissed his way down her neck. Her little gasp of pleasure made him swell with triumph.

More. He wanted more.

He stroked her breast through the thin muslin of her frock, palming and kneading her softness. Her nipple tightened. He strummed the sensitive peak, brushing his thumb back and forth in a teasing caress. She moaned faintly, and he covered her mouth with his own, drinking in the sound of her pleasure.

When the kiss ended, he readied an insincere apology.

I was carried away, didn't mean to press you too far, we'll go as slowly as you please, et cetera…

But she spoke first.

"Sebastian." She wet her lips. "Make love to me tonight."

Mary held her breath as she gazed into his eyes.

Sebastian was silent for so long, she began to grow self-conscious. And confused. He'd just explored her body as shamelessly and thoroughly as a Viking plundering a medieval village. How could he be shocked by her request?

He shook his head. "It's too soon."

"We're married. This is our honeymoon," she said. "Once we leave, you'll have your business affairs, I'll be settling into a new home. There seems no better opportunity than now."

In fact, she worried that this might be the only opportunity. If they didn't forge a strong connection before leaving Kent, she might be waiting a very long time for another chance.

"It's only been one day," he said. "You're not over your disappointment."

"I told you, I didn't love him. Perhaps I ought to be heart-sick, but I'm not. I'm relieved."

"That doesn't mean you're ready to leap into bed with me."

"No doubt it will be awkward the first time. But that's always going to be the case, no matter how long we wait." She turned her gaze around the empty beach. "Besides, there's little else to do for amusement. Unless you'd rather play cards all night."

He groaned. "Playing cards with you is like trying to hold back the tide—there's no way to win."

"Fair enough," she said. "No cards. Which brings us back to bed."

He stared into the distance.

"Sebastian, even though I wasn't expecting to wed you, I've always found you attractive."

In fact, she'd never grasped the strength of that attraction until she realized how her feelings toward Giles paled in compari-son. Giles didn't make her hot all over with just a simple glance. He didn't even make her lukewarm.

She hesitated. "Of course, I don't expect you to say you feel similarly about me."

He caught her chin and tilted her gaze to his. "You," he said darkly, "make me ache with wanting."

Oh.

Sweet heavens. She'd known he'd say something kind. He'd compliment her eyes, maybe, or possibly her complexion. Call her pretty, perhaps. But his intense confession of desire had caught her entirely unawares.

She'd gone fishing for a few small compliments, and some-how she'd harpooned a whale.

He took her by the arms. "I know you enjoy arguing, but this is one matter where I will not be moved. We had a rushed wedding, but we're not going to rush this. I've too much pride to make it a hurried, joyless affair. I'm going to learn every inch of your body, and you're going to learn every inch of mine. And when I know you're ready…when you're aching for me every bit as fiercely as I'm aching for you…that's when I'll make love to you. Not a moment before."

Oh, Sebastian. That won't require nearly so much effort as you think.

Her own body needed no further coaxing. But how was she going to convince *him?*

"We'd better go back." He turned them in the direction of the cottage and offered his arm. "Dick and Fanny are preparing us a proper dinner, I'm told. Four courses, to be served in the dining room."

"Oh, my. I think they're scrambling to please you so they can remain in your employment."

"As well they should be."

As they neared the cottage, they spied a coach coming up the lane.

"It's here. Thank God." Sebastian strode toward the house with renewed vigor.

"Whose coach is that?"

"It's mine. I sent an express from Canterbury, telling my housekeeper I'd be here. I asked her to send the carriage with some of my belongings from Town."

Mary lingered behind him as he went to greet the coachman. Together, the two men unstrapped a trunk from the back of the carriage. Sebastian carried it inside, undid the latches, and opened it.

"It's a miracle. I am now in possession of clean shirts, a razor, shaving soap and tooth powder… All the modern necessities of a civilized life." To her, he added, "And *we* have a coach and driver.

We can go wherever you like. If Ramsgate doesn't suit you, you may have your choice of destination. Bath. The Wye valley. The Lake district. The Cotswolds. Hell, why not Paris?"

Mary laughed at his last suggestion. Inside, her feelings were conflicted.

She was running out of excuses to stay in this cottage. She loved this place, but she had to admit she would love it better after a few months of repairs and deep cleaning. And to be truthful, she'd always wanted to see the Cotswolds.

But what she wanted more than anything was to prevent Sebastian from pulling away. He'd made it clear that he felt compelled by honor to observe an irrational, indefinite waiting period before they consummated their marriage. And yet he'd confessed to desiring her, just now.

You make me ache with wanting.

A shiver traveled from her scalp to her toes.

Knowing Sebastian as well as she did, Mary could easily guess what self-sacrificing compromise he'd arrived at to ease his conscience. He'd keep his distance from her, in whatever way he could. Sleeping in separate beds. Pursuing different interests. Burying himself in whatever work he could find.

"We can't leave until after dinner," she said. "Dick and Fanny will be sorely disappointed, after going to all that work."

"The horses need to be watered and fed, as well."

Mary gathered her courage. "You're now in possession of evening attire. And I have a full trunk of gowns I've never had the chance to use. Since Mr. and Mrs. Cross have promised us a formal dinner, why don't we dress accordingly?"

"If you like." He scratched his jaw. "I need a bath and a shave, anyway. Shall we say dinner in an hour, then?"

"Perfect."

Chapter 8

While Mary disappeared upstairs to bathe and dress, Sebastian adopted the study as his own dressing chamber. He took more care with his appearance than he had on the day he'd been presented at Court. He scrubbed, lathered, shaved, combed, brushed, dressed, and buttoned. He even polished his boots to a mirror gleam. Beau Brummel he was not, but he didn't want to let Mary down.

He'd always thought it a shame that she never had a proper Season in London. It wasn't something her father could have afforded, he supposed. The Claytons were an established and well-respected family, but the second son of a fourth son of a landed gentleman didn't come into much, if any, inheritance. So no social debut for Mary, and now she'd missed her own wedding day—which was meant to be a bride's chance to shine.

She deserved to have been admired by scores of gentlemen, on any number of occasions. Life and circumstance had prevented it. So Sebastian was going to smarten up, stand at the bottom of those stairs, and admire her enough to equal a hundred men put together.

Almighty God.

Perhaps a thousand men put together.

She descended the stairs in a shimmering gown of sapphire blue that precisely captured the brilliant hue of her eyes. Pearls studded the elegant upsweep of her auburn hair, in much the same way that charming freckles dotted the pale shelf of her décolleté.

"You're beautiful," he said, stating it as a simple fact. Because it was.

Her blue eyes widened with surprise. But she shouldn't have been surprised.

"I've always thought you were beautiful. From the first time I saw you."

"Oh, come now. I won't believe that. I was your best friend's irritating older sister."

"You were my best friend's irritating and *beautiful* older sister. And I was the typical adolescent boy, unable to think about anything else. There were summers when just being in the same room with you nearly drove me out of my skin."

Her eyes softened. "I never knew you admired me like that."

"Oh, I admired you." He looked her over. "I admired you a great deal, and often. Sometimes more than once a day."

She gave him a playful punch on the shoulder. "Se-*bas*-tian Lawrence Ives."

By God, he was a selfish bastard. She'd spent more than an hour readying herself for his eyes alone, and all he wanted was to turn her about, lead her straight back up to the bedchamber, and give her a ravishing that would undo all her effort in a matter of seconds.

Sebastian dragged his thoughts back to proper gentlemanly behavior. He should not, would not make love to her tonight. He would banish the thought entirely.

Naturally, the next words from her mouth were, "I notice you assembled the bed."

So much for banishment.

He took her hand, bowed over it, and kissed her fingers. "Lady Byrne. May I have the honor of escorting you in to supper?"

"Thank you, Lord Byrne. You may."

⁓

Mary sent up a quiet prayer as he led her into the dining room, where the table had been set with the finest chipped plates and mismatched cutlery the cottage had to offer.

Please, let this work.

The gown seemed to have been a good start. If Dick and Fanny had managed a dinner that was the tiniest bit romantic, and if she plied him with a few glasses of wine, perhaps he would set down those shields composed of misplaced duty and loyalty, just for the night.

To the side of the room, Dick stood at ramrod-straight attention, holding a rather shabby-looking towel draped over his left forearm. His coat was buttoned, and he'd tied a red kerchief about his neck as a cravat. A severe part divided his hair into unequal halves—save for an errant cowlick that bounced with every mild stirring of the air.

He bowed deeply at the waist. "Milord. Milady."

"Good evening, Mr. Cross," Mary said, as Sebastian helped her into her chair. "This all looks so lovely. You and Mrs. Cross must have worked very hard."

"Oh, aye." Dick poured wine into their glasses. "But we're not afraid of hard work, milady. Never did you meet such devoted servants as me and my Fanny."

Sebastian reached for his wine, clearly sensing the theme of the dinner unfolding. *One-Hundred-and-One Reasons Not to Sack Your Caretaker.*

Dick brought out a tureen and a woven basket, over which had been draped a small square of linen. "Yer first course, milord and milady. Soup and pain."

"Soup and *what?*" Sebastian echoed.

"Pain." Dick ladled soup into Mary's bowl.

Mary looked at the greasy beef broth. Then she met Sebastian's inquiring gaze and shrugged in response. *I have no idea.*

"Don't make no sense to me either, milord. But the missus says everything's French tonight." He waggled his fingers in a mocking gesture. "La-di-dah."

As he left, he whisked the cloth off the basket between them, revealing the contents.

Bread. Or, as the French would call it, *pain.*

"Oh, dear." Mary pressed a hand to her mouth. "This does not bode well."

"Let's just eat." Sebastian raised his spoon and sipped from it once, then set it down. "On second thought, let's not eat this." He nodded in her direction. "How do you find the pain? Tolerable?"

"Stop," she pleaded. "Don't make me laugh. They'll hear it."

Once the soup had been cleared away, Dick returned with a covered oval platter, which he placed on the table with a flourish. Mary crossed her fingers and her toes, hoping for better this time.

"Second course, milord and milady. Poison." He bowed. "Enjoy."

After Dick had retreated, Mary stared at the covered platter. "Tell me he didn't say 'poison'."

"I believe he did." Sebastian tilted his head. "Do we dare lift the dome for a peek?"

"I'm not looking. You look."

"Maybe we should just ask for more pain instead."

"Oh, you." She plucked a roll from the basket and lobbed it at him. "I'll give you pain."

He lifted a finger to his lips. "Shh."

In the kitchen, Dick and Fanny could be heard having a squabble of their own.

"Woman, what do ye have me sayin' out there? Servin' poison to his lordship."

"I told ye, 'tis right here in the cookery book. P-O-I-S-S-O-N. Poison. That's what they call it."

"Oh, aye. That's what the Frenchies *want* ye to believe. *That's* how they get you."

Sebastian lifted the lid from the platter, revealing precisely what they both now expected: a steamed fish.

"Voila," he said. *"Poisson."* He reached for the fillet knife. "Shall I serve you some, my lady?"

"You try it first."

"I *am* known for living dangerously." He took a bite. Chewed. Sat a moment in thought. "It's not poisoned. But it's also not good."

By the time Dick returned with the third course, the dining room was thick with suspense. In lieu of eating, Sebastian and Mary had spent the past several minutes placing bets on what disastrous dish they'd be served next.

"'Ere we are." Dick plunked two shallow serving bowls on the table. "Stewed chicken and mash."

"Really?" Well, that was disappointing.

"Cocky vein!" Fanny stormed out from the kitchen. "Lord above ye, man. How many times did I say it. It's cocky vein and pumpery." She swept her husband with a withering glance. "Have a bit of class, ye old fool."

"Oh, I'm the fool, am I?" Dick followed her back into the kitchen, carrying on in a loud voice. "Yer the one what'll have us sacked before I even serve the chocolate mouse."

The shouting and arguing continued, interspersed with the banging of pots and pans.

Cringing, Mary poked at the *coq au vin* and gave the dish of *pommes purée* a cautious stir. It was the consistency of paste.

So much for a romantic dinner.

"Perhaps we'd be better off in Ramsgate after all," she said, resigned. "I'd best pack my things. Do you think they'd notice if we just slipped upstairs?"

"Not for another hour or two, at least." He threw down his serviette. "Come along, then. Let's make our escape."

Together, they crept up the stairs to the bedchamber and shut the door behind them. Once they were alone, she couldn't help but laugh. "The worst part of it is, I'm so hungry."

"Take heart. If we make haste, we're less than an hour's drive from a proper meal."

She turned her back to him. "Will you help me with the buttons and laces? I need to change for the journey."

He hesitated. "I'm not adept with those things."

"I'm sure you'll manage."

He hadn't been joking about his ineptitude. As he plucked at the hooks and wrestled with the buttons, Mary was strangely encouraged. It was comforting to know he hadn't amassed *too* much practice disrobing women.

Once he had the back of her gown undone, the tapes of her petticoats unknotted, and the laces of her stays untied, he stepped back a few paces. "There you are. I'll step out into the corridor while you—"

"Don't be silly."

She turned around, hastily shoving her gown and petticoats to the floor, and setting aside her corset. She stepped out from the mound of silk and crinoline, standing before him in only a lacy, light blue chemise. One she'd taken in at the seams an inch here and there, so that it clung to her breasts and hugged her hips.

Mary pulled the pins from her hair one by one, then shook

59

out her upsweep with a sensuous toss of her head. A motion that not coincidently pushed her breasts high.

She'd come this far. She might as well be completely shameless. Neither wifely homemaking or romantic dinners had succeeded in changing his mind. She had only one strategy left: seduction.

And she had absolutely no idea what she was doing.

His reaction wasn't quite what she'd been hoping for. He frowned at her body as though it were an arithmetic problem he couldn't solve.

"What is it? Don't you like what you see?"

"I can't say that I do, not entirely. You're a vision of beauty, but you're standing there in a negligee meant for your honeymoon with another man."

"Oh, is that the problem?"

She slipped the chemise over her shoulders and drew her arms out of the sleeves. The garment dropped to the floor in a lacy puddle.

"There," she said. "No more negligee. Problem solved."

Chapter 9

No, Sebastian thought to himself.

No, his problem was definitely not solved. His problem was growing by the moment, hardening against the placket of his trousers.

"Don't play games," he warned, keeping his distance a few paces away. "If you don't truly want this…"

"I want this." She crossed to him, reached for his hand, and placed it on her breast. "I want you."

That was it.

Restraint, depleted. Argument, over. Decision, made.

There was only so much temptation a man could take from the woman who'd been the center of his every torrid fantasy. If she wanted him, she was going to get him. Every last, aching inch.

He grabbed her by the backside and lifted her straight off the floor so that her legs wrapped around his hips. Then he carried her toward the bed.

"Wait," she said. "Are you sure it will hold us?"

In answer, he simply tumbled with her onto the mattress. She tensed and held her breath.

When the bed didn't collapse, he arched an eyebrow in chastisement. "You know, you should have a little more faith in your husband."

"You're right. In the future, I will."

"Good."

She didn't need to know that the bed was now sturdy because he'd followed her instructions. He'd keep that to himself.

Now that he had her beneath him, he brushed a light kiss to her lips and then trailed his mouth downward, making an arrow-straight path for her hardened left nipple.

He'd been waiting more than a decade to taste her there.

He swirled his tongue over the tight pink peak, and then drew her nipple into his mouth, suckling her lightly. She bucked and moaned beneath him, and he pulled harder still. He transferred his attention to the other breast, licking over her nipple and then painting her breast in widening circles.

She was so soft, so sweet. He could have spent a full night treasuring and nuzzling her bosom alone—and someday, he vowed, he would—but tonight, his body clamored with impatience for more.

He rose up on his knees to yank at his cravat and wrestle out of his topcoat. She helped him in the effort, unbuttoning his waistcoat and tugging his shirt free of his trousers. When he was finally bared to the waist, he lowered himself atop her. His blood sang when their bodies met, skin to skin.

He slid a hand down her body, reaching between her thighs to explore her silken heat. She gasped and bit her lip. He held her gaze as he caressed and explored. With his thumb, he covered the swollen bundle of nerves at the crest of her sex, rubbing gently back and forth. Her breathing quickened, and her eyes glazed with pleasure.

"Good?" he asked.

She nodded. "Very."

He bent his head to kiss her neck, then dipped lower to her breasts and belly, making his way to her mound.

Her thighs clamped down on his shoulders. "Wait."

Sebastian waited. He'd waited more than a decade already. What were a few minutes more?

She pushed up on her elbows, looking down at him. "What are you doing?"

"I mean to kiss you." He pressed his thumb against her. "Here."

"Are you—" She broke off, distracted by his touch. "Are you sure?"

"Yes." He clucked his tongue. "Not three minutes ago, you promised to have a little more faith in your husband."

"I should know better than to say such things." She lay back and flung her wrist over her eyes. "Very well. Do what you like."

He smiled with devilish intent. "I'm going to do what you'll like, too."

When he laid his mouth to her...well, to *her*...Mary nearly jumped out of her skin. The pleasure was so keen, so unspeakably bright. One flutter of his tongue against her most sensitive place, and she writhed beneath him.

The sweetest torture.

Within moments, he had her responding to him with startling intensity. Her pleasure mounted at an unprecedented pace. She began to gasp and moan, lifting her hips to seek more contact. Then he slid a finger inside her, and the blissful stretch sent her over the edge. She cried out and convulsed with release. Her intimate muscles pulsed around his finger.

When the pleasure had left her wrung out and panting, he slid back up her body. He reached between them to unbutton the falls of his trousers. Then he found her hand and brought it to his erection. "Touch me."

She explored his full length with her fingertips. The softness, the ridges, the smooth skin at the tip, and the hardness that underpinned everything. She encircled his shaft, stroking lightly up and down. His resulting moan was immensely gratifying.

He lowered himself atop her, and she felt the broad crown of his erection prodding at her entrance. "Are you ready?" His voice was hoarse, strained.

She nodded, unsure if it was the truth.

He pressed against her, and then inside her, stretching her body to accommodate his. She winced with the pain of it, but tried not to cry out. The last thing she wanted was for him to stop.

He loved her in slow, gentle, steady strokes. Even when his arm muscles trembled with tension, and his breathing was harsh. He took care of her, guarding her even from the strength of his own need.

Until the very end, when his pace faltered for a moment. When he resumed, it was in a faster, harder rhythm. His gruff, masculine sounds of pleasure thrilled her. She clutched his shoulders tight.

With a final, deep thrust, he collapsed atop her, shuddering with release.

Afterward, they held each other tight. No talking or kissing. Just breathing and existing together in the most simple, essential of ways.

He drew in a deep breath and released it as a growl, wrapping his arms around her and squeezing tight. "You."

She smiled. "You."

He lay back on the bed, and she rested her head on his chest.

"It's quiet downstairs," she said. "Fanny and Dick stopped arguing."

"Do you think they killed each other with rolling pins, or

poisoned themselves?"

"More likely they went out to the stables and fell asleep. But whichever it was, I hope they cleaned the kitchen first."

As he held her, tenderly stroking her hair, Mary's conscience began to needle her. "There's something I should tell you," she said, hoping he'd take the revelation well. "Something I should have told you before we married."

"There's something I should have told you, too."

"What's that?" She was happy for him to go first.

"I want a family. I should have told you this before you agreed to elope with me. But it's not only that I need an heir. I want our child—hopefully, our children—to have a true home."

Oh, Sebastian.

He rolled onto his back and stared up at the ceiling. "My youth was a string of broken promises. You know that. You were there. How many Christmases did I spend at your house when my own father failed to collect me from school?"

"I don't know. But we were always happy to have you."

"You pitied me," he said. "The worst part was, you expected my presence, every year. Always a place set at the table, small gifts wrapped and waiting. Packets of sweets, fishing lures. I always assumed you scavenged a few odds and ends from about the house to give me, so that I wouldn't feel left out. Until the year you knitted me a muffler. You probably don't recall."

"Of course I do. I made Henry one, as well."

"I still have it, you know. Blue and gold stripes, my house colors at school. That's when I finally understood. A muffler in my house colors couldn't have been produced on a moment's notice. You had to have knitted it in advance, and you had it wrapped and waiting."

"Sebastian..."

"You knew. You all knew what I didn't want to believe. That

my father's excuses were inventions, and his promises meant nothing. He would never keep his word to come for me. I should have realized it myself." He passed a hand over his face. "I'd never felt so stupid."

Mary sat up in bed. "You should not have felt stupid," she told him. "You were a boy who wanted to believe in his father. There's no shame in that. I'm only sorry he never lived up to your hopes."

"You can't know how it feels. It's like being tied to a cartwheel, tumbling from hope to disappointment over and over again. Eventually, your spirit is simply crushed. I won't put a child through that." His eyes met hers. "Can you understand?"

She nodded.

"So it's not enough for me to simply sire an heir and be done with it. I want to be a good father. To be there for every Christmas, every birthday. Teach our children to ride and fish, patch up their scrapes, put them to bed at night. I know it's more than I let you believe when we eloped. I was selfish. Because I knew if I had any chance at that life, it would have to be with you. If you not for you and Henry and your father, I wouldn't know what family is."

"You darling man." She leaned over and kissed his lips. "Nothing would make me happier than a family with you. Nothing."

"You're certain?"

"Have you ever known me to be otherwise?"

"I suppose not." His mouth tipped in a lopsided smile. "So what was it you wanted to tell me?"

She stroked the space between his eyes. For once, there was no furrow in his brow, and she couldn't bear to carve a new one.

"I wanted to tell you that I love you."

His expression shuttered. "You don't have to say that."

"I think I do have to say it. Because I've been keeping it to myself for years now, and it's burning a hole in my chest. You don't believe me, do you?"

He shook his head. "Not for a moment. That is, unless you mean it in some sort of friendship or fondness way. There are different sorts of love, and—"

"Wait." She sat up in bed, reaching for the edge of the rumpled bed linens. "I'll prove it to you. You know I worked on my trousseau for years. Every girl does. But I hemmed this particular set of bed linens the year I was one-and-twenty, I believe." She skimmed her fingertips along the side until she found what she was searching for. "Here." She showed it to him. "What does that say?"

He peered at it. "I don't know."

"Yes, you do. It's 'M.C.I.' I was dreadfully infatuated with you by that time, and in a sentimental moment, I embroidered your initial at the end of my own. Nearly seven years ago."

"But you say you were infatuated. Infatuation isn't love."

"No, it's not. I told myself the same thing. So after you'd purchased your commission and left for war, I put my feelings aside. I told myself to be practical. Giles asked to court me, and then he asked me to marry him. I said yes. Even though I knew I didn't love him, could never love him."

She closed her eyes and steeled herself. "But it wasn't until I lost Henry that I truly knew. The rector came to call. And I knew—I just knew—it meant one of you had been killed. When he told me Henry had died, I was devastated. Not only because I'd lost him—but because I'd had this terrible flash of relief in the same moment. I'd thought, Thank God it wasn't Sebastian." A hot tear fell to her cheek, and she impatiently dashed it away. "Can you imagine? I hated myself. But after that, there was no denying it. I was truly in love with you."

He caught her in his arms and rolled them over, so that she was beneath him. His disbelieving gaze searched hers. "Mary."

"I love you." She took his face in her hands and kissed his cheek. "I love you." Then his chin. "I love you." Then the pounding pulse under his jaw. "I love y—"

He covered her mouth with his, kissing her forcefully. As if to forbid her from loving him, and at the same time beg her to never, ever stop. They tangled tongues and limbs and hearts and souls.

He buried his face in her neck. "I need you," he whispered hoarsely. "Can you take me again?"

She nodded. "Yes."

This time it was different. Not slow and tender, but desperate, urgent. He raised up on his arms and stared down at her, never breaking his intense gaze as he took her in deep, powerful thrusts.

This wasn't lovemaking. It was possession.

"You're mine now," he said through clenched teeth. "Do you hear me? You're mine."

He moved harder, faster. As if he meant to pound at her body until he became part of her, sharing the same blood and bone, and pulling away would tear them both in two.

She held him tight, arching her hips to match his rhythm. His every motion drove her higher. Closer to her peak. Closer to him.

Somehow they found each other in the feverish storm of climax, holding each other in every possible way.

He slumped atop her, and she caressed his hair and shoulders as he recovered his breath. His back was slick with sweat.

"You're mine now," he whispered. "Don't even try to argue it."

"I won't argue it," she said. "Just as long as you understand that you're mine, too."

Chapter 10

They woke to the sound of someone pounding at the cottage's front door.

Mary sat up in bed. "Who on earth could that be, at this hour? Surely not Dick or Fanny."

Sebastian gave a derisive chuckle. "*Certainly* not Dick or Fanny. They would never knock."

"You have a point."

"It would seem they've gone away," he said after a minute. "We can go back to sleep."

"I don't know if I can return to sleep. Not after being startled awake."

"Well, then." He slid his arm around her, drawing her close. "I suppose we could amuse ourselves in some other way."

The pounding resumed.

With a groan, Sebastian let his head drop to the pillow. "Stay here. I'll see to it." With a light kiss to her lips, he rose from the bed and slid his legs into a pair of breeches. He plucked his shirt from where it lay discarded on the floor and dragged it over his head and arms. Then he reached for the candlestick and stumbled his way down the stairs.

"Whoever you are," he bellowed as he slid back the bolt, "you had better have a good reason for knocking at my door in the middle of the night."

He opened the door.

"Believe me, I have an excellent reason." Giles Perry stood on the threshold, holding a lantern in his left hand. He wore a dark cape flung over his shoulders and a murderous expression on his face. "I've come to do this."

He drew back his fist and punched Sebastian square in the ribs.

Oof. The blow took Sebastian by surprise. But that was about all it did. Perry hadn't the bulk or strength to deliver a bruising punch. Sebastian didn't even reel a step backward. Looking into Perry's pitifully disappointed face, he almost felt a bit sheepish about his lack of response. He wondered if perhaps he ought to double over and feign a dramatic groan just to be polite.

But then he recalled that this was the man who'd left Mary waiting at the altar—and Sebastian had no further inclinations to pity.

"How dare you come here," he growled.

"How dare you *be* here," Perry replied, indignant.

"This is my house. I've every right to be here."

"You don't have any right to be here with *her.*" Perry ducked under Sebastian's arm and entered the cottage. "I've come to rescue Mary."

"Rescue her from what? A surfeit of orgasms?"

"From you, you…rutting blackguard."

Oh, now that was too much. "Listen, you puling jackass. You have no claim on Mary any longer. That ended when you abandoned your promises and left her waiting at the altar alone. The only reason you don't have a bullet hole through your chest is because she begged me to spare your miserable life."

"What are you on about? I didn't abandon her."

"I'm fairly certain you did. I was there, and you weren't."

"Because I honored her request. Mary broke it off. Not me."

"You lying little—"

"He's not lying." Mary stood at the top of the stairs, dressed in one of his shirts. "He's telling the truth. I'm the one who called the wedding off."

Sebastian shook his head in disbelief. "That can't be. It doesn't make any sense."

Perry moved to confront her directly. "You ran away with this brigand? Willingly?"

"He's not a brigand. How did you find us here?"

"The coachman told me, when he finally returned. I'd hired that carriage by the hour, I hope you know." He shook his head in irritation. "This was supposed to be a discreet agreement. You become a spinster, I get a seat in the House of Commons."

"You'll still be an MP. It's not as though you need to win votes. You're buying a rotten borough. With my dowry, I might add."

Sebastian couldn't have heard that correctly. "You gave him your dowry?"

"Yes." She descended the remainder of the stairs. "In exchange for releasing me from the engagement on such late notice."

"I should have never agreed," Perry said. "I've a promising future in Parliament, you know. I could be Prime Minister one day. Many people are saying it. When this news gets about, you will have made me the laughingstock of London."

"Oh, Giles. Please. No one thinks about you half as much as you believe they do."

"I beg your pardon. I'm in the newspapers at least twice a year."

"You're a man, from an influential family. You'll weather the scandal, buy your seat in Parliament. From there you can make your reputation in politics—and, I might add, a far better match. If anything, people will believe you had a close escape. They'll assume it was my fault, and that you were well rid of me."

Sebastian pinched the bridge of his nose. "Help me out here, Mary. If you'd called off the wedding that morning, why did you come to the church? With all your belongings packed, no less?"

She looked everywhere but at him.

"Oh my God. You *planned* this?"

"In a way. I couldn't be certain you'd suggest we elope. But I prepared for it, just in case you did."

"You told me you didn't *want* to elope. You argued against it."

"I argue against everything. It's in my blood." She bit her lip. "If I'd agreed too easily, you might have been suspicious."

He turned away, pushing a hand through his hair. "This is unbelievable."

"I'm so sorry. It was wrong of me. But for a year now, I've been so worried about you. You never called on me anymore. I realized I couldn't go through with the wedding months ago and—"

"Months ago?" Perry squawked.

Sebastian wheeled to face him. "Why are you even still here?"

"Because." Perry tugged on his waistcoat. "I believe I'm owed an apology, too."

"You're sure as hell not getting one from me."

"I'm sorry, Giles." Mary approached him. "Truly sorry. I should have broken it off ages ago. But I would have done you a greater disservice by becoming your wife. I think we both know that we weren't suited to one another."

"Perhaps not, but—" Perry made a disgusted gesture in Sebastian's direction. "Of all men, did it have to be him?"

"Yes." She glanced at Sebastian. "Of all men, it had to be him."

Emotion gripped his heart like a fist.

"You heard my lady," he said to Perry. "Now you can leave. Go back to London and amuse yourself by further corrupting Parliament."

Perry finally moved to leave the cottage. "I'll have you know," he said, hand on the door latch, "that I have several plans for the benefit of the poor and infirm."

"Just get *out.*"

At last, the man was gone.

Sebastian turned to his deceitful bride.

She clutched her hands together in front of her. "I owe you a great many explanations."

"You can offer all the explanations you like, but there is no excuse for this."

"Will you at least hear me out?"

First, he had a few things to say of his own. "You lied to me. You led me to believe you were jilted, alone, vulnerable. When Henry and I went off to war, I made a vow to protect you if he didn't come back. The past few days, I've tortured myself. Knowing that I kept that promise to guard you as best I could, and at the same time believing it came at the cost of your happiness. Now I learn that was only a falsehood. How much of the rest of it was lies, too?"

"None of it. I swear. Everything else was the truth." She approached him. "I know I lied about being jilted. That was wrong of me. But if you care for me, and want to raise a family together... Is it really so terrible to learn that it was you I loved all along?"

"I don't know if I can believe that now."

He could scarcely believe those three words when she'd spoken them the first time. How the hell was he supposed to accept them now?

"You think I would lie to you? About the day I learned of my own brother's death?" Her voice shook with emotion. "If that's how little you think of me, we can annul the marriage. No one knows we went through with it, save for the coachman and Giles. And Dick and Fanny, but who would they tell?"

"The Church knows. I know. We said vows. We've had…" He motioned impatiently. "…marital relations."

Well, look at that. He'd come up with a polite term all on his own.

"A marriage can be annulled on grounds of fraud," she said. "If that's what you allege, I won't fight it."

"Oh, I'll be damned if I'll annul this marriage. You're not getting off that easy." He inhaled slowly, trying to steady himself. "I'm far from a perfect man. But if there's one thing I value above all else, it's keeping my promises."

"I know that."

"Precisely, Mary. You know that. You *know* that. And you used it against me."

She nodded slowly. "You're right, I did. I see that now. Perhaps it is unforgivable."

She turned and quietly climbed the stairs.

Sebastian didn't follow her.

Mary spent the rest of the night pacing, weeping, and hoping against hope that she might hear his footfalls on the steps. That he might come to her, allow her to apologize, consider giving her another chance.

Before Giles had arrived, they'd been on the verge of something truly wonderful. And because of her stupidity, she'd set them back years. She didn't know how she'd convince him to trust her again. But no matter how long it took, she wouldn't give up.

As dawn broke, she finally heard the sounds of stirring downstairs. She ran to the door and pressed her ear against it, holding her breath.

No footfalls.

Instead, she heard the sound of carriage wheels crunching on the gravel drive. Heading away.

No.

Mary looked about the room, panicked. Good Lord, she was still barefoot and dressed in nothing but his shirt. She hadn't been able to bring herself to change out of it.

There was no time to find something else.

She flew from the room, hurrying down the stairs on bare feet and reeling around a corner in her mad dash for the front door. "Sebastian! Sebastian, wait! Don't le—"

Oof. As she opened the door, she collided with something.

Something tall and strong and wonderful.

"Sebastian." She threw her arms about his neck and hugged him tight. "Thank God you're still here. I thought you'd left me."

"I told you I wouldn't leave you. What would make you think that?"

She pulled back and searched his eyes. "The coach. I heard it leaving."

"Ah, yes. That would have been Dick and Fanny making their departure."

"You don't mean that you sacked them? I know they're terrible, but they meant well."

"I did not sack them," he said. "I've sent them away on holiday. To Ramsgate."

She blinked at him, stunned. "Sebastian, you didn't."

"I did. They're to have a room at the finest establishment, with full board and all expenses paid, for a week. And we"—he put his hands on her waist—"are on our own."

"Just the two of us?"

He nodded.

"For a whole week?"

"I'm afraid so." He shook his head, as if in dismay. "We'll have to prepare our own food. Split our own wood. Nothing to do but stroll on the beach in the afternoons and sit by the fire in the evenings with a glass of wine." His eyes darkened. "Well, that and go to bed early."

"Oh, dear. What a trial." She put her hand to his cheek. "Does that mean you've forgiven me?"

"I'm not sure. I'm still put out with you, and I spent the whole night thinking on it. You lied to me."

"I know."

"But then, you also gave up your dowry and the chance at a secure marriage, risking ruin and spinsterhood for me. Which seems as though it ought to count for something, too."

"I only did it because I loved you so much. I hoped perhaps you felt something for me, but I knew you'd never do anything about it. If I told you how I felt, you would have fled as quickly as Shadow could carry you. You would never have married me unless you believed you were coming to my rescue."

"I wish I could contradict that, but I suspect you're right."

"I'm always right."

He gave her a look.

"Often right," she amended. "If it helps, my first plan didn't feature deceit at all. I was going to simply seduce you. But I didn't have the confidence that I could pull it off."

His mouth quirked at the corner. "Oh, you could have pulled it off."

"Really?"

"Without a doubt." He drew her close, resting his forehead to hers. "Mary, Mary. Can you truly love me that much?"

"More. You should have seen my third plan if this one didn't work. There were highwaymen."

He laughed.

It was a warm, unburdened laugh that made her heart soar.

She'd disarmed him now. He couldn't keep her out any more.

"I love you," he murmured. "God, it feels good to say that at last. I love you, Mary."

He bent to kiss her, then stopped. "I've just thought of something. If your trunks weren't packed for a honeymoon with Giles Perry, does that mean all those negligees were truly—"

"For you?" She smiled. "Yes."

"Are there more of them?"

"Take me upstairs and find out."

She didn't have to ask twice. He bent down, lashed an arm around her thighs, and flung her over his shoulder before mounting the stairs.

Mary hoped he'd pieced that bed together correctly. Because it would be put to the test all week long.

Epilogue

"Come away from the window, darling," Mary said. "You're leaving nose prints on the glass."

Henry pouted. "You said Papa would be here in time for tea."

"He will be. He promised, and your father always keeps his promises."

Mary was eager for Sebastian to arrive, too. Tending all four of their children during his absence had left her frayed at the edges. When they were in London or at Byrne Hall, she had a nursemaid to help, but when they took their annual holiday here in the cottage, they preferred to keep it family only. With the addition of Dick and Fanny Cross, of course.

She shifted Molly, her youngest, to the other arm and wiped the spittle from her chubby face. The poor dear was cutting a new tooth. At least William had gone upstairs for a nap, but Jane and Henry wouldn't cease bickering.

Someday, Mary would finish her latest strident letter to the editor of *The Times*—but it wouldn't be today.

"Papa will most likely be late," Jane said.

"No, he won't."

"He will be. On account of the rain."

"It's not raining," Henry objected.

"Not now, not here. But it was raining hard an hour ago. The clouds have shifted since. So it's likely raining on him now. He may even have to stop over somewhere."

Mary shushed them both. "He'll be here. He'd never miss one of your birthdays."

"It's an easy enough promise to keep, considering three of our birthdays are all in the same month. Henry's the only one left out." Jane crinkled her nose in thought. "It's rather a coincidence, isn't it?"

Mary only smiled. It was no coincidence at all that three of their four children had been born in March. Not when one considered that they spent a holiday at the Kentish seaside every June.

There was just something about that bed.

Mary dearly hoped she wasn't around when Jane finally puzzled out the truth. She was far too clever, that one.

She set Molly down on the floor to play, then invited Henry to sit on her lap. "Henry, have I told you about the night you were born?"

Jane rolled her eyes. "Only hundreds of times."

Mary ignored her eldest's complaint and wrapped her arms around Henry. "You came early. I was at Byrne Hall, and your Papa was in London. I sent a message to him by express, but I thought he couldn't possibly arrive before you did. I should never have doubted. Your father rode all night—in the rain, mind—and arrived just in time to welcome you into the world. He was there for your first birthday, and he'll be here to see you turn six. Never doubt it."

Molly pressed a sticky hand to the window. "Papa!"

"See?" Henry gave his older sister a superior look. "I told you he'd be here in time for tea."

"And I told you it was raining," she replied.

Sebastian came through the door, dripping with rainwater and stamping the mud from his boots. "I heard there's a young master here who's six years of age. Who could that be?"

"It's me!" Henry rushed to give his father a hug.

He was closely followed by Jane.

Molly toddled over and made grabby hands. "Papa, up."

William scrambled downstairs, rubbing the sleep from his eyes, and jumped on his father's back.

Mary exchanged amused glances with her husband. "You look like a children tree."

An exceedingly handsome children tree. Even all these years later, he never failed to take her breath away.

"Come have cake, Papa."

"Can we go sea-bathing tomorrow?"

"Did you bring us sweets from Town?"

"Papapapapapa."

She came to his rescue, shooing them away. "Give your father a rest, all of you. Go help Mrs. Cross set the table for tea."

Once they'd all run off, she was finally able to greet Sebastian with a kiss of her own. "In case you couldn't tell, you were very much missed." She helped him out of his coat. "Was the road terrible?"

"Shadow and I have been through worse."

"I'm so glad you're here. Your children are exhausting."

He chuckled. "I'll take them down to the seaside tomorrow so you can have a rest."

"You don't have to do that."

"Oh, I do." His arms went around her, and his voice went dark. "You're going to need a rest tomorrow, because I mean to keep you up late tonight."

The kiss he gave her was one of boundless love and intense passion, and it conveyed an unmistakable message:

She'd better not make any plans for next March.

A Note from the Author

Thank you so much for reading! I hope you enjoyed *His Bride for the Taking*. If you feel so inclined, please recommend this book to a friend or post an honest review. Recommendations and reviews help other readers find new books to enjoy.

Keep turning pages for a peek at my latest books!

The best way to receive updates on new releases is to sign up for my email newsletter at:

tessadare.com/newsletter-signup

How the Dukes Stole Christmas
A Christmas Romance Anthology

From the ballrooms of London, to abandoned Scottish castles, to the snowy streets of Gilded Age New York, four bestselling authors whip up unforgettable Christmas romance.

"Meet Me in Mayfair" by Tessa Dare
Louisa Ward needs a Christmas miracle. Unless she catches a wealthy husband at the ball, the Duke of Thorndale will evict her family from their home. When Louisa finds herself waltzing with the heartless Thorndale, she's unnerved by his handsome looks— and surprising charm.

"The Duke of Christmas Present" by Sarah MacLean
Rich and ruthless, Eben, Duke of Allryd doesn't care for the holidays. But when Lady Jacqueline Mosby returns to town after a long absence, Eben falls under the spell of Christmas—and the woman he never stopped loving.

"Heiress Alone" by Sophie Jordan
When Annis Bannister finds herself stranded in the Highlands during a Christmas snowstorm, she must fend off brigands terrorizing the countryside. Her only hope falls on her neighbor, a surly hermit duke who unravels her with a kiss.

"Christmas in Central Park" by Joanna Shupe
Mrs. Rose Walker pens a popular advice/recipe column. No one knows Rose can't even boil water. When her boss, Duke Havemeyer, insists she host a Christmas party, Rose must find a husband, an empty mansion, and a cook. But Rose fears her plan is failing—especially when Duke's attentions make her want to step under the mistletoe with him.

Give yourself a holiday gift. Order *How the Dukes Stole Christmas* now!

Available Now

The Wallflower Wager
(Girl Meets Duke, Book 3)

They call him the Duke of Ruin.
To an undaunted wallflower, he's just the beast next door.

Wealthy and ruthless, Gabriel Duke clawed his way from the lowliest slums to the pinnacle of high society—and now he wants to get even.

Loyal and passionate, Lady Penelope Campion never met a lost or wounded creature she wouldn't take into her home and her heart.

When her imposing—and attractive—new neighbor demands she clear out the rescued animals, Penny sets him a challenge. She will part with her precious charges, if he can find them loving homes.

Done, Gabriel says. How hard can it be to find homes for a few kittens?
And a two-legged dog.
And a foul-mouthed parrot.
And a goat, an otter, a hedgehog . . .

Easier said than done, for a cold-blooded bastard who wouldn't know a loving home from a workhouse. Soon he's covered in cat hair, knee-deep in adorable, and bewitched by a shyly pretty spinster who defies his every attempt to resist. Now she's set her mind and heart on saving him.

Not if he ruins her first.

Turn the page for an excerpt from *The Wallflower Wager*.

The Wallflower Wager
Chapter One

Over her years of caring for unwanted animals, Lady Penelope Campion had learned a few things.

Dogs barked; rabbits hopped.

Hedgehogs curled up into pincushions.

Cats plopped in the middle of the drawing room carpet and licked themselves in indelicate places.

Confused parrots flew out open windows and settled on ledges just out of reach. And Penny leaned over window sashes in her nightdress to rescue them—even if it meant risking her own neck.

She couldn't change her nature, any more than the lost, lonely, wounded, and abandoned creatures filling her house could change theirs.

Penny gripped the window casing with one hand and waved a treat with her other. "Come now, sweeting. This way. I've a biscuit for you."

Delilah cocked her plumed head and regarded the treat. But she didn't budge.

Penny sighed. She had no one to blame but herself, really. She'd forgotten to cover the birdcage completely at sundown, and she'd left a candle burning far too late while she finished a delicious novel. However, she'd never dreamed Delilah could be clever enough to reach between the bars with one talon and unlatch the little door.

Once the parrot had escaped her cage, out the window she

flew.

Penny pursed her lips and whistled. "See, darling? It's a lovely biscuit, isn't it? A gingersnap."

"Pretty girl," the parrot chirruped.

"Yes, dear. What a pretty, pretty girl you are."

Delilah made a tentative shuffle sideways. At last, progress.

The bird came closer . . .

"That's it. Here you come, sweetheart."

Closer . . .

"Good girl."

Just a few more inches . . .

Drat.

Delilah snatched the biscuit from Penny's fingers, scuttled backward, and took a brief flight, coming to land on the windowsill of the next house.

"No. Please. No."

With a flutter, Delilah disappeared through the open window.

Drat and blast.

The old Wendleby residence had lain vacant for years, save for a few servants to watch over the place, but the property had recently changed hands. The mysterious new owner had yet to make an appearance, but he'd sent an architect and a regiment of laborers to make several noisy, dusty improvements. A house under construction was no place for a defenseless bird to be flying about in the dark.

Penny had to retrieve her.

She eyed the ledge connecting the two houses. If she kicked off her slippers, climbed out onto the ledge, clung to the narrow lip of mortar with her bare toes, and inched across it . . . the open window would be within reach. The distance was only a few feet.

Correction: It was only a few feet to the window. It was twenty-odd feet to the ground.

Penny believed in a great many things. She believed that education was important, books were vital, women ought to have the vote, and most people were good, deep down. She believed that every last one of God's creatures—human or otherwise—deserved love.

However, she was not fool enough to believe she could fly.

She tied her dressing gown about her waist, jammed her feet into slippers, and padded downstairs to the kitchen, where she eased open the top-left drawer of the spice cabinet. Just as she remembered, all the way at the back of the drawer, affixed to the wooden slat with a bit of candle wax, was a key.

A key that opened the Wendlebys' back door.

Penny removed the ancient finger of metal and flaked away the wax with her thumbnail. Her family and the Wendlebys had exchanged keys decades ago, as good neighbors were wont to do. One never knew if an urgent situation might arise. This counted as an urgent situation. At this hour, waking the staff would take too much time. Delilah could fly out the way she'd entered at any moment. Penny could only hope that this key still fit its proper lock.

Out into the night she went. In one hand, she carried Delilah's empty cage. With the other, she drew her dressing gown tight to keep out the chill.

Skulking past the front door of the house, she made her way down to the servants' entrance. There, obscured by shadows, she slid the key into the lock, coaxing it past the tumblers. Once she'd inserted it all the way, she gave the key a wrenching twist.

With a click, the lock turned. The door fell open.

She paused, breathless, waiting for someone inside to raise the alarm.

There was only silence, save for the thudding of her heart.

Here she was, a complete stranger to criminal activity, about to commit prowling, or trespassing, or perhaps even burglary—if not some combination of the three.

A faint whistle from above underscored the urgency of her mission.

Closing the door behind her, Penny set the birdcage down on the floor, dug into the pocket of her dressing gown, and withdrew the taper and flint she'd stashed there before leaving her house. She lit the slender candle, lifted Delilah's brass cage with the other, and continued into the house.

She made her way through the servants' hall and up a flight of stairs, emerging into the house's main corridor. Penny hadn't been in this house for several years now. At that time, what with the Wendlebys' reduced circumstances, the place had fallen into a state of genteel decay.

At last, she beheld the result of several months' construction.

If the new owner wanted a showplace, he had achieved one. A rather cold and soulless one, in her opinion. But then, she'd never been one for flash. And this house not only flashed—it blinded. The entrance hall was the visual equivalent of a twenty-four-trumpet fanfare. Gilded trim and mirrored panels caught the light from her candle, volleying the rays back and forth until they were amplified into a blaze.

"Delilah," she whispered, standing at the base of the main staircase. "Delilah, where are you?"

"Pretty girl."

Penny held her candle aloft and peered upward. Delilah perched on the banister on the second-floor landing.

Thank heaven.

The parrot shifted her weight from one foot to the other and cocked her head.

"Yes, darling." Penny took the stairs in smooth, unhurried

steps. "You are a very, very pretty girl. I know you're grieving your mistress and missing your home. But this isn't your house, see? No biscuits here. I'll take you back home where it's warm and cozy, and you shall have all the gingersnaps you wish. If you'll only stay . . . right . . . th—"

Just as she came within an arm's reach, the bird flapped her wings and ascended to the next landing.

"Pretty girl."

Sacrificing quiet in favor of speed, Penny raced up the steps and arrived on the landing just in time to glimpse the parrot dart through an open doorway. She was sufficiently familiar with the house's arrangement to know that direction would be a blind end.

She entered the room—a bedchamber with walls recently covered in lush silk damask and anchored by a massive four-poster bed. The bed was large enough to be a room unto itself, and cocooned by emerald velvet hangings.

Penny quietly shut the door behind her.

Delilah, I have you cornered now.

Cornered, perhaps, but not yet captured.

The bird led her on a chase about the room, flitting from bedpost to wardrobe to bedpost to mantel to bedpost—Heavens, why were there so many bedposts?

Between racing up the stairs and chasing about the room, Penny was out of breath. If she weren't so dedicated to saving abandoned creatures . . .

Delilah alighted on the washstand, and Penny dove to rescue the basin and ewer before they could crash to the floor. As she replaced them, she noticed several other objects on the marble table. A cake of soap, a keen-edged razor, a toothbrush and tooth powder. Evidence of recent occupation.

Male occupation.

Penny needed to catch that parrot and flee.

Instead of perching on a bedpost, Delilah had made the mistake of flying beneath the canopy. Now she found her escape stymied by the voluminous draperies.

Penny rushed toward the bed, took a flying leap, and managed to grasp the parrot by one tiny, taloned foot.

There. I've got you.

Catching the parrot would have been a triumph to celebrate. However, as her luck would have it, Penny immediately found herself caught, too.

The chamber's connecting door swung open. A candle threw light into the room. She lost her grip on Delilah's leg, and the bird flapped out of reach once again—leaving Penny sprawled across a stranger's bed in her nightclothes, birdless.

As she turned her head toward the figure in the doorway, she sent up a prayer.

Please be a maid.

Of course she could not be so fortunate. A man stood in the connecting room doorway. He was holding a candle, and wearing nothing at all.

Well, he wasn't truly naked, she corrected. He was clothed in *something*. That "something" was damp scrap of linen clinging so precariously to his hips that it could slide to the floor at any moment—but it qualified as clothing of a sort.

And everyone was naked beneath their clothing, weren't they? This wasn't so different. Why be missish about it? After all, he didn't look embarrassed. Not in the least.

No, he looked magnificent. Magnificently irate.

"Where the hell did you come from?"

His tone of voice was understandably angry. It was also knee-erasing.

Penny scrambled out from the bed hangings and all but tumbled to the floor. "I'm from next door. Where I live. In my house."

"Well, I own this house."

"I didn't realize the new owner was in residence."

"As of this evening, I am."

"Yes. So I see."

She saw a great deal. Far more than was proper. Yet she couldn't tear her gaze away.

Lord, but he was a big, beautiful beast of a man.

There was just so much of him. Tall, broad, powerfully muscled. And utterly bare, save for that thin bit of toweling and his thick, dark hair. He had a great deal of hair. Not only plastered in damp curls on his head, but defining the hard line of his jaw. And lightly furring his chest.

He had nipples. Two of them.

Eyes, Penny. He has two of those, too. Focus on the eyes.

Sadly, that strategy didn't help. His eyes were chips of onyx. Chips of onyx dipped in ink, then encased in obsidian, then daubed with pitch, then thrown into a fathomless pit. At midnight.

"Who *are* you?" she breathed.

"I'm Gabriel Duke."

Gabriel Duke.

The Gabriel Duke?

"Pleased to make your acquaintance," she said out of habit, if only because she could hear her mother tut-tutting all the way from India.

"You shouldn't be pleased. No one else is."

No, they weren't. The papers had exhausted an ocean of ink on this man, who came from unknown origins and now possessed untold influence. Ruthless, said some. Shameless, said others. Sinfully wealthy, agreed all.

They called him the Duke of Ruin.

From somewhere above, Delilah gave a cheeky, almost sala-cious whistle. The parrot swooped out from beneath the bed hangings and flew all the way across the room, alighting on an unused candle sconce on the opposite wall. Placing herself directly behind Penny's new, impressively virile neighbor.

Oh, you traitorous bird.

He flinched and ducked as the parrot swept overhead. "What the devil was that?"

"I can explain."

I just don't particularly want to.

"It's a parrot," she said. "My parrot."

"Right. And who are you, again?"

"I . . . erm . . ." Her hands couldn't decide where to be. They merely displayed the panicked desire to be anywhere else.

Water dripped from some hard, slick part of his body, count-ing out the beats of her mortification.

Drip. Drip. Drip.

"I'm Lady Penelope Campion."

Lady Penelope Campion.

The Lady Penelope Campion?

Gabe tilted his head to one side, shaking the last bit of bath-water from his ear. He could not have heard her correctly. Surely she meant to say she was a *servant* in the house of Lady Penelope Campion.

"You can't be Lady Penelope."

"I can't?"

"No. Lady Penelope is a spinster who lives alone with dozens of cats."

"Not *dozens*," she said. "A touch over *one* dozen at the moment, but that's only because it's springtime. Kitten season, you know."

No, he didn't know. None of this made any sense whatsoever.

Lady Penelope Campion was the main reason he'd acquired this property. New-money families would pay outrageous amounts to live next door to a lady, even if said lady was an unappealing spinster.

How on earth was *this* woman a spinster? She was an earl's daughter, surely possessed of a large dowry. If none of the title-hungry, debt-ridden layabouts in Mayfair had seen fit to propose marriage, simple logic dictated there must be something remarkably off-putting about her. An unbearably grating voice, perhaps. A snaggletooth, or poor personal hygiene.

But she displayed none of those features. She was young and pretty, with no detectable odor. Her teeth were a string of pearls, and she had a voice like sunshine. There was nothing off-putting about her whatsoever. She was . . . on-putting, in every way.

Good God, he was going to sell this house for a bloody fortune.

Assuming the lady wasn't ruined, of course.

At her level of society, being ruined didn't take much. Strictly as a random example, she could be ruined by being found alone and scarcely clothed in the bedchamber of the aristocracy's most detested, and currently most naked, villain.

"You need to leave," he said. "At once."

"I can't. Not before retrieving—"

"Wait here. I'm going to dress, and then I'll see you home. Discreetly."

"But—"

"No argument," he growled.

Gabe had clawed and climbed his way out of the gutters,

using the ruined aristocrats of London as stepping stones along his way. But he hadn't forgotten where he came from. He'd learned how to talk and walk among people who would think themselves his betters. But that lowborn street urchin still lived within him—including the rough cutpurse voice that had genteel ladies clutching their reticules. When he chose to use that voice, it seldom went unheeded.

Lady Penelope Campion wasn't paying attention at all.

Her gaze was focused on something behind him, over his shoulder. He instinctively began to turn his head.

"Stop," she said with perfect calm. "Don't move."

He heard a strange flutter, and in the next moment it happened.

A bird landed on his shoulder. A parrot, she'd said? The creature's toes prickled along his skin. His muscle twitched with the urge to shrug it off.

"No, don't," she said. "I'll come for her."

Usually, Gabe would balk at taking orders from a lady—or from anyone else. However, this was a decidedly unusual situation.

"Pretty girl," the bird squawked.

Gabe set his jaw. *Do you think I haven't noticed that, you cursed pigeon with pretensions?*

She crept toward him, padding noiselessly over the carpet, step by silent step. And as she came, sweet words fell from her lips like drops of raw honey.

"That's it, darling," she murmured.

The fine hairs on the back of his neck lifted.

"Stay . . . right . . . there."

The hairs on his arms lifted, too.

"Yes," she breathed. "Just like that."

Now she had the hairs on his calves involved. Damn it, he

had too many hairs. By the end of this they would all be standing at attention.

Along with other parts of him.

"Don't stir," she said.

He couldn't speak for the parrot, but Gabe was doing some stirring. One part of him had a mind of its own, especially when it came to beautiful women in translucent chemises. He hadn't lain with a woman in some time, but his body hadn't forgotten how.

He couldn't help himself. He stole a glance at her face. Just a half-second's view. Not long enough to pore over every detail of her features. In fact, he didn't get any further than her lips. Lips as lush as petals, painted in soft, tender pink.

She was so close now. Near enough that he when he breathed, he inhaled a lungful of her scent. She smelled delicious. A faint hunger rose in his chest.

"I know you're feeling lost. And not a little frightened. You miss her terribly, don't you? But I'm here, darling. I'm here."

Her words sent a strange ache spreading from his teeth to his toes. A painful awareness of all his hollow, empty places.

"Come home with me," she whispered. "And we'll sort out the rest together."

He couldn't take any more of this. "For God's sake, get the damned thing off me."

At last, she collected the feathered beast. "There we are." Cradling it her arms, she carried the parrot to its birdcage and tucked it within.

Gabe exhaled with relief.

"She'd settle more if I covered her cage," his beautiful intruder said. "I don't suppose you have a towel?'

He glanced at the linen slung about his hips. "How badly do you want it?"

Her cheeks flushed. "Never mind. I'll be going."

"I'm going to walk you."

"Truly, you needn't do that. It's only next door. No more than twenty paces down the street."

"That's twenty paces too many."

Gabe might not operate by polite society's rules, but he understood them sufficiently to know this situation violated at least seventeen of them. And anything that damaged her reputation would decrease the profit he stood to collect on this house.

Until he sold this property, her worth was intertwined with his.

"You're no doubt accustomed to having your way, Your Ladyship. But I've ruined enough lords, baronets, knights, and gentlemen to fill the whole of Bloom Square." He arched an eyebrow. "Believe me when I say, you've met your match."

Want to read on? Get *The Wallflower Wager* today!

More Books by Tessa Dare

Girl Meets Duke series
The Duchess Deal
The Governess Game
The Wallflower Wager
The Bride Bet (coming in 2020)

Castles Ever After series
Romancing the Duke
Say Yes to the Marquess
When a Scot Ties the Knot

Spindle Cove series
A Night to Surrender
Once Upon a Winter's Eve
A Week to be Wicked
A Lady by Midnight
Beauty and the Blacksmith
Any Duchess Will Do
Lord Dashwood Missed Out
Do You Want to Start a Scandal

The Stud Club series
One Dance with a Duke
Twice Tempted by a Rogue
Three Nights with a Scoundrel

The Wanton Dairymaid series
Goddess of the Hunt
Surrender of a Siren
A Lady of Persuasion

Novellas
His Bride for the Taking
"Meet Me in Mayfair", in How the Dukes Stole Christmas
The Scandalous, Dissolute, No-Good Mr. Wright
How to Catch a Wild Viscount

About the Author

Tessa Dare is the *New York Times* and *USA Today* bestselling author of more than twenty historical romances. Blending wit, sensuality, and emotion, Tessa writes Regency-set romance novels that feel relatable to modern readers. Her books have won numerous accolades, including Romance Writers of America's prestigious RITA® award (twice) and the *RT Book Reviews* Seal of Excellence. *Booklist* magazine named her one of the "new stars of historical romance," and her books have been translated worldwide.

A librarian by training and a book-lover at heart, Tessa makes her home in Southern California, where she lives with her husband, their two children, and a trio of cosmic kitties.

To receive updates on Tessa's new and upcoming books, please sign up for her newsletter:
www.tessadare.com/newsletter-signup

Facebook: facebook.com/tessadareauthor
Twitter: @tessadare
Instagram: @tessa_dare
Website: http://www.Tessadare.com

Made in the USA
Monee, IL
02 December 2020